DRIVING
HER CRAZY

AMY ANDREWS

This book is for all women out there who have ever looked in the mirror and headed straight for the chocolate/wine/Tim Tams. And for men with rose-coloured glasses.

PROLOGUE

SADIE BLISS'S breath caught at the emotive image. Wandering through the ritzy New York gallery surrounded by a crowd of A-listers who blinged and glittered so much it hurt her eyes, she was stopped in her tracks by its starkness.

The background murmur of voices and clinking of champagne glasses faded as the world shrank to just the photograph, the centrepiece of the exhibit.

Mortality.

She'd seen it already, of course, in *Time* magazine, but there was something so much more immediate about it this close. As if it had just been snapped. As if the tragedy were unfolding before her eyes.

She felt as if she were standing in the daunting arid landscape, weighed down by the heat perfectly captured as it shimmered like a mirage from the sand. Smelling the jet fuel from the twisted Black Hawk carcass that she'd seen in the other shots. Hearing the cries of the young soldier as he clutched one bloody hand to his abdomen and reached the other rosary-beaded one into the impossibly blue sky. Calling for someone. God maybe? Or his girlfriend?

Watching his tears turning the grime on his face to muddy tracks. Tasting his despair as life faded from his eyes.

The caption beneath said: *Corporal Dwayne Johnson, nineteen, died from fatal wounds before help could arrive.*

Goosebumps needling her skin, tears pricking at her eyes brought Sadie back to the here and now. She moved on wishing she'd never been given the coveted ticket to the much anticipated opening night of Kent Nelson's *A Decade of Division.* All the pieces snapped from the award-winning photojournalist's lens were disturbing, but this image, known throughout the world, was particularly harrowing.

A portrait of a young man facing death.

A private moment of anguish.

And although the artist in her appreciated the abstract prettiness of the rosary beads against the bright blue dome of a foreign sky, the image was too intimate—she felt as if she was intruding.

Sadie pushed through the crowd out of the gallery into the sultry June night. She needed a moment. Or two.

CHAPTER ONE

Four months later...

KENT NELSON stood staring across at the view of Darling Harbour, his gaze following the line of the iconic white sails of the Sydney Opera House. He stood with his back to the woman swinging idly in her chair, his good leg planted firmly in front of the other as he leaned into the hand resting high against the floor to ceiling tinted window.

'So, let me get this straight,' Tabitha Fox said, tapping her pen on her desk, her bangles jangling, as she too admired the view. Not the one she was used to seeing when she looked towards her windows but a mighty fine one nonetheless. 'You want to *drive* several thousand kilometres to take a few photos?'

Kent turned, his ankle twinging as he rested his butt against the glass, and folded his arms across his chest. 'Yes.'

Tabitha frowned. She'd known Kent a long time, they'd been to uni together about a thousand years ago, even shared a bed for a while, but since the accident in Afghanistan he'd been practically invisible.

Until he'd turned up today wanting to take pictures any staff photographer could take.

'Okay...why?'

Kent returned her curious gaze with a deliberately blank one of his own. 'I'm your freelance photographer—it's what you pay me for.'

Tabitha suppressed a snort. His official status might be freelance photographer for the glossy weekend magazine *Sunday On My Mind,* but they both knew he'd 'declined' every job offered and, she'd bet her significant yearly salary, probably hadn't taken a photo since the accident.

She narrowed her eyes at him as she tried to see behind the inscrutable expression on his angular face. 'There are these things called planes. They're big and metal and don't ask me how but they fly in the air and get you to where you want to go very quickly.'

A nerve kicked into fibrillation along his jaw line and Kent clenched down hard. 'I don't fly,' he pushed out through tight lips.

The words were quiet but Tabitha felt the full force of their icy blast. Cold enough to freeze vodka. She regarded him for a moment or two as her nimble brain tried to work the situation to her advantage. She drummed her beringed fingers against her desk.

An outback road trip. Local people. The solitude. The joys. The hardships. The copy laid out diary style.

And most importantly, breathtaking vistas capturing the beauty and the terror in full Technicolor shot by a world-renowned, award-winning photographer on his first job since returning from tragedy in Afghanistan.

For that reason alone the paper would sell like hot cakes.

'Okay.' Tabitha nodded, her mind made up. 'Two for the price of one. Journey to the Red Centre stuff—the most spectacular photos you can take.'

'As well as the Leonard Pinto feature?'

She nodded again. 'Might as well get my money's worth

out of you. Lord knows when you'll grant us some more of your time.'

Kent grunted. Tabitha Fox was probably the most business-savvy woman he'd ever met. She'd built *Sunday On My Mind* from a fluffy six-page pull-out supplement to a dynamic, gritty, feature-driven eighteen-page phenomenon in five years.

He lounged against the glass for a moment. 'Tell me, I'm curious. How'd you get him? Pinto? He's pretty reclusive.'

'He came to me.'

Kent raised an eyebrow. 'A man who shuns the media and lives in outer whoop-whoop came to you?'

Tabitha smiled. 'Said he'd open up his life to us—nothing off limits.'

Kent fixed her with his best *'and pigs might fly'* look. 'What's the catch?'

'Kent, Kent, Kent,' she tutted. 'So cynical.'

He shrugged. After spending a decade in one war zone or other, cynical was his middle name. 'The catch?' he repeated.

'Sadie Bliss.'

Kent frowned. The journo on the story with the most spectacular byline in the history of the world? 'Sadie Bliss?'

Tabitha nodded. 'He wanted her.'

Kent blinked. 'And you agreed?' The Tabitha he knew didn't like being dictated to. She especially didn't like relinquishing her editorial control.

She shrugged. 'She's young and green. But she can write. And, I—' she smiled '—can edit.'

Kent rubbed a hand along his jaw. 'Why? Does she know him?'

'I'm not entirely sure. But he wanted her. So he got her.

And so did you. She can…' Tabitha waved her hand in the air, her bangles tinkling '…navigate.'

Kent narrowed his gaze. 'Wait. You want her to travel with me?' Three thousand kilometres with a woman he didn't know in the confines of a car? He'd rather be garrotted with his own camera strap.

Not happening.

Tabitha nodded. 'How else am I going to get my road trip story?'

Kent shook his head. 'No.'

Tabitha folded her arms. 'Yes.'

'I'm not good company.'

Tabitha almost burst out laughing at the understatement. 'In that case it'll be good for you.'

'I go solo. I've always gone solo.'

'Fine,' Tabitha sighed, inspecting her fingernails. 'Sadie and her *staff* photographer can fly to Pinto and get the job done in a fraction of the time and at half the cost and you can go back to your man-cave and pretend you work for this magazine.'

Kent felt pressure at the angle of his jaw and realised he was grinding down hard. He'd already burned his bridges at a lot of places the last couple of years. He was lucky Tabitha was still taking his calls after the number of times she'd covered for him.

But days in a car with a woman whose name was Sadie Bliss? She sounded like a twenty year old cadet whose mother had named her after one too many fruity cocktails.

'I do believe,' Tabitha said, swinging in her chair as she prepared to play her ace, 'you owe me a couple.'

Kent shut his eyes as Tabitha called in his debts. 'Fine,' he huffed as he opened them again because he wanted— needed—to do this. To get back into it again.

And he did owe her.

Tabitha grinned at him like the cat that got the cream. 'Thank you.'

Kent grunted as he strode to her desk, barely noticing his limp, and sat down. 'Do you like his nudes?'

Tabitha nodded. 'I think he's sublime. You?'

Kent shook his head. 'They're all too skinny. Androgynous or something.'

Tabitha rolled her eyes. 'They're ballet dancers.'

Leonard's nude of Marianna Daly, Australian prima ballerina, had won international acclaim for his work and hung in the National Gallery in Canberra.

'Well, they're not Renaissance women, that's for sure.'

Tabitha raised an elegantly plucked eyebrow. 'You like Rubenesque?'

Kent grunted again. 'I like curves.'

Tabitha smiled. *Oh, goody.* She picked up the phone her gaze not leaving his. 'Is Sadie here yet?' She nodded twice still spearing Kent with her Mona Lisa smile. 'Can you send her in?' she asked, replacing the receiver before the receptionist had a chance to respond.

Kent narrowed his gaze. 'I don't trust that smile.'

Tabitha laughed. 'Suspicious as well as cynical.'

Kent had no intention of subjecting himself to her Cheshire grin. He rose from the chair and prowled to the window, resuming his perusal of the view as the door opened.

Sadie checked her wavy hair was still behaving itself constrained in its tight ponytail as she stepped into the plush corner office, determined not to be intimidated. So what if the legendary Tabitha Fox could make grown men weep? She'd given Sadie the job and, lowly cadet reporter or not, she knew her big break when she saw it.

Even if Leo's agenda was questionable.

'Ah Sadie, come in.' Tabitha smiled. 'I'd like you to

meet someone.' She nodded her head towards Kent. 'This is your photographer, Kent Nelson.'

Sadie turned automatically, her gaze falling on broad shoulders before her brain registered the name. She blinked.

'*The* Kent Nelson?' she asked his back, the image that had affected her a few months ago revisiting.

Kent shut his eyes briefly. Great. *A groupie.* He turned as Tabitha said, 'The one and only.'

Sadie was speechless. Multi-award-winning, world-acclaimed photojournalist Kent Nelson was coming with her to the back of beyond to take photos of a reclusive celebrity?

She almost asked him who he'd pissed off but checked her natural urge to be sarcastic.

Kent was pretty damn speechless himself as one look at Sadie Bliss blew his mind. And his was not a mind easily blown. Tabitha was smirking in his peripheral vision so he hoped he wasn't staring at her like a cartoon character whose eyes had just popped out on springs because, try as he might, he was powerless to pull his gaze away from all those curves.

Curves that started at her pouty mouth and *did not let up.*

Sure, she'd tried to contain them in her awful pin-striped suit but they looked as if they were going to bust out at any moment. They looked as if they had a mind of their own.

Bliss? *Very appropriate.* A man could starve to death whilst lost in those curves and not even care.

Great. Just what he needed. Three days in a car with a rookie reporter whose curves should come with a neon warning sign.

Sadie looked at Tabitha with a scrunched brow. 'I'm

sorry, I don't understand…*Kent Nelson* is the photographer on my story?'

'We-e-ll-ll…' Tabitha wheedled. 'Plans have changed a little.'

Sadie could feel the pound of her pulse through every cell in her body as a sinking feeling settled into her bones.

They wanted to take her off the story.

Give it to someone else.

Sadie cleared her throat. 'Changed?'

She was determined to act brisk and professional. She might not have scored this story on merit, but she intended to show everyone she had the chops for feature writing. And if Ms Tabitha bloody Fox thought she wouldn't fight for her story, then she was mistaken.

Sunday On My Mind, the country's top weekend magazine supplement, was exactly where she wanted to be.

And if she had to write one more best-dog-in-show story she was going to scream.

'We want you to do two stories. The feature on Leonard. And another.' Tabitha flicked her gaze to Kent briefly before refocusing on the busty, ambitious brunette who had been bombarding her inbox with interview requests for the last three months. 'On an outback road trip.'

Sadie held herself tall even though inside everything was deflating at the confirmation that the story was still hers. She didn't even allow herself the tiniest little triumphant smile as Tabitha's words beyond '*two stories*' sank in.

'A road trip?'

She looked at Kent, who was watching her with an expression she couldn't fathom. She was used to men gawking at her. Being lumbered with an E cup from the age of thirteen had broken her in to the world of male objectification early. But this wasn't that. It was brooding. Intense.

He was intense.

She'd seen pictures of him before, of course. The night of the exhibition there'd been a framed one of him taken on location somewhere in a pair of cammo pants and a khaki T-shirt. His clothing had been by no means tight but the shirt had sat against his chest emphasising well-delineated pecs, firmly muscled biceps and a flat belly.

His light brown hair had been long and shaggy—pushed back behind his ears. His moustache and goatee straggly. He'd been laughing into the lens, his eyes scrunched against the glare, interesting indentations bracketing his mouth.

He'd held a camera with a massive lens in his hands as if it were an extension of him. As a soldier carried a gun.

The whole rugged, action-man thing had never been a turn-on for her—she preferred her men refined, arty, like Leo—but she'd sure as hell been in the female minority that night in New York.

Hell, had the man himself been there, she doubted he would have left alone.

But looking at him today she probably wouldn't have recognised him if they'd passed in the street. Gone was the long hair and scraggy goatee that gave him a younger, more carefree look. Instead he was sporting a number-two buzz cut, which laid bare the shape of his perfectly symmetrical skull and forehead. His facial hair had also been restricted to stubble of a number-two consistency, emphasising the angularity of his cheekbones and jaw, shadowing the fullness of what she had to admit was a damn fine mouth, exposing the creases that would become indentations when he smiled.

If he smiled.

The man sure as hell wasn't smiling now. He had his arms folded beneath her scrutiny and Sadie became aware suddenly she was watching his mouth a little too indecently. Quickly, she widened her gaze out.

Unfortunately it found a different focus. The way his folded arms tightened the fabric of his form-fitting, grey turtle-neck skivvy across the bulk of his chest. The bunch of muscles in his forearms, where the long sleeves had been pushed up to the elbows.

'Yes,' Kent said smoothly, interrupting her inspection. 'A road trip.'

He watched as Sadie took that on board with eyes as remarkable as the rest of her. Finally he understood what people meant when they talked about doe-eyed. They were huge, an intense dark grey, framed with long lashes. They didn't need artfully applied shadow or dark kohl to draw attention—they just did.

His gaze drifted to the creamy pallet of her throat, also bare of any adornment. In fact, running his gaze over her, he realised Sadie Bliss was a bling-free zone. No earrings, no necklaces, no rings.

In stark contrast to Tabitha there was nothing on Sadie's person that sparkled or drew the eye.

Not an ounce of make-up.

Not a whiff of perfume.

Even her mouth, all red and lush, appeared to be that way all on its own merit.

Sadie cleared her throat as his gaze unnerved her. An odd little pull deep down inside did funny things to her pulse and she glanced at Tabitha to relieve it.

'From Darwin to Borroloola? That's like…a thousand kilometres.'

Sadie did not travel well in cars.

Tabitha shook her head but it was Kent who let loose the next bombshell. 'Actually, it's Sydney to Borroloola.

You can fly from Borroloola to Darwin and then back to Sydney once the interview is done.'

Sadie forgot all about the funny pull, Kent's celebrity status and the good impression she was trying to make with Tabitha. 'Are you nuts?' she said, turning to face him. 'That would have to be at least...' she did a quick mental calculation '...three times the distance!'

Kent remained impassive at her outburst although it was refreshing to hear a knee-jerk, unfiltered opinion for once instead of one couched in the usual kiss-arse afforded to his level of celebrity. Tarnished as it was.

Did she honestly think he wanted to spend three days in a car with her? But he knew Tabitha well enough to know that she was an immovable force when her mind was made up.

'Three thousand, three hundred and thirteen kilometres to be precise.'

Sadie felt nauseated at the mere thought. 'And we're not flying because...?'

Kent didn't blink. 'I don't fly.'

'It'll be great,' Tabitha enthused, jumping in as Kent's voice became arctic again. 'You and Kent. A car. A travel diary. The Red Centre. The true outback. Journalism at its most organic.'

Sadie gave Tabitha a look that suggested she was probably also certifiable. 'But that will take days!'

'Let me guess,' Kent drawled, amused by her horrified demeanour. 'City girl, right?'

Sadie looked back at him. 'No,' she denied, despite the fact that she was an urban creature to her core. Fast lane, city lights, cocktail bars and foreign film festivals.

'I just get really, really car sick.' It sounded so lame when she said it out loud but she doubted the great Kent

Nelson would tolerate stopping every two minutes so she could hurl up her stomach contents.

Kent's jaw tightened again. *Great.* Three days in a car with a city chick and her weak constitution.

It just kept getting better.

'I guess that's why they invented motion sickness medication,' he said woodenly.

Sadie shook her head vigorously. 'Oh, trust me, you do *not* want to be around me when I'm on that. I get totally trippy. It is not pretty.'

Kent raised an eyebrow. Vomiting or tripping. Sounded like a trip forged in hell.

Maybe another place, another time in his life he would have been more than happy to see Little-Miss-Curvy getting trippy. But now just the thought was plain annoying.

'Thanks for the heads up,' he said.

'This could be a great opportunity for you, Sadie,' Tabitha interjected. 'Two feature stories for the price of one. Of course, if you don't think you're up to it we can always find someone else...'

Sadie wanted to stamp her foot at the not-so-subtle ultimatum. But she didn't. Tabitha was right. It *was* a gift. How was her boss to know about Sadie's nervousness at facing her ex-lover again? Or that when she did, she wanted to look a million dollars, not like a wrung-out dish mop?

At least a gruelling car journey would help the crash diet she'd put herself on since finding out about this opportunity two days ago. The last time she'd seen Leo, she'd been thin, her curves straitjacketed by a strict eating regime.

Not naturally svelte, she had taken a while to slim down when they'd first started their relationship. But Leo's love and encouragement had been a fantastic incentive. Every time he'd raved about the symmetry of her prominent collar, wrist and hipbones, or the way the milkiness of her skin stretched sparingly over the hard surfaces beneath, she'd felt accomplished.

He used to stroke her hair as it fell in between the angles of her bony scapulas and tell her it looked like rippling satin flowing between a sculpted valley. That her creamy skin was the perfect foil.

The only thing curvy about her then had been her breasts. And, no matter how much Leo had lamented them, not even rigid dieting had had an effect on their size. He'd offered to pay for a reduction and she'd been thrilled at the suggestion. Thrilled that the brilliant artist had seen something special in her body. Seen it as a work of art, an empty canvas.

Thrilled that she'd become his muse, revelling in his almost obsessive need to paint her.

She was excruciatingly aware now she was not the woman he had sent away. That he had loved.

And she had a lot to prove.

So there was one upside to this proposed nightmare road trip. Between starvation and puking up constantly she could lose a stone or two before seeing him again.

'No. It's fine,' she said, briskly pulling herself out of the food-obsessing habits of a past life. 'I can do it. I just can't promise the upholstery of the hire car will ever be the same again.'

'No hire car,' Kent said. 'We'll be using my all-terrain vehicle.'

Sadie nodded at him. *Of course*. An all-terrain vehicle. Mr Intense-and-rugged probably also had the Batmobile tucked away somewhere.

'When do we leave?' She sighed.

'I'll pick you up in the morning. Pack light. No places serving drinks with umbrellas where we're going.'

'Gee,' she said sweetly, 'imagine my surprise.'

Sadie's fallback position had always been sarcasm—a defence mechanism against a world that constantly misjudged her because of the size of her chest. As an adult she tried her best to contain it but, sadly, it was too ingrained in her nature to be completely stifled.

And if Kent Nelson insisted on this ridiculous road trip, on spending days in a car alone together, then he could consider this a heads up.

Tabitha might have forced her hand, but she didn't have to like it.

Sadie was ready when Kent rang the doorbell the next morning. She was wearing loose denim cut-offs and a modest polo shirt, her hair fell freely around her shoulders and a pair of ballet flats completed the ensemble. Her medium-sized backpack and a small insulated bag were waiting at the door.

Kent blinked at the transformation from serious city career girl in a power suit to girl-next-door. Again, her clothes did nothing to emphasise the curves—if anything they were on the baggy side.

It was just that Sadie's curves were uncontainable.

Dressed like this, still absent of any bling, it was easy to believe she was only the twenty-four years Tabitha had informed him of yesterday.

Which made her precisely twelve years younger than him.

She was a baby, for crying out loud.

'What's in here?' Kent asked as he grabbed the fridge bag off her and lifted her pack. An hour ago he'd been whistling as he'd loaded the vehicle for the trip, a buzz he hadn't felt in a long time coursing through his veins.

The buzz was still there.

He just wasn't sure, in the presence of Sadie, if it was one hundred per cent related to the drive any more.

'Ginger ale,' she said, watching how the muscles in his tanned forearms bunched.

Before yesterday she would have admired the delineation, the symmetry, the beauty of the fluid movement. Today they just made her insides feel funny.

And that was the last thing she needed.

Her insides would feel funny enough the minute they hit the first bend in the road.

'I don't expect you to carry my stuff,' she said testily.

She wasn't some delicate elfin thing that would shatter if she picked up anything heavier than her handbag. One look would have told him that. But he was already striding away despite a rather intriguing limp.

From the crash, she assumed.

She followed at a more sedate pace, glancing at the sturdy-looking Land Rover parked on the road with trepidation. With its functional metal cab, sturdily constructed roof railings and massive bull bar it looked like something the Australian army had engineered for land and amphibious combat. And had been test driven in a pigsty if the sludge-and-muck-encrusted paint job was any indication.

Staring at the tank on wheels, Sadie absently wondered whether Kent Nelson was compensating for something.

'I didn't know you could get mud masks for cars,' she murmured as she joined him at the open back doors.

Kent grunted as he rearranged the supplies to accommodate her backpack. 'She's not young, she's not very pretty but she'll do the job.'

Sadie preferred pretty.

And men who didn't talk about cars as if they were female. Especially this car. *This car was one hundred per cent male.*

'Does *she* have air conditioning?'

Kent nodded. He held up the cool bag. 'You want this up front?' he asked.

'Thanks.'

She took it from him as he shut the doors and noticed a muddy sticker supporting a Sydney football team near the handle and another for an Australian brewery. He looked like a man who knew his way around a ball. And a beer.

Leo had drunk gin.

Kent looked down on her. The morning sun fell on the pale skin of her throat and he noticed the pulse beating there. 'Got your pills?' he asked gruffly.

She patted her bag. 'At the ready.'

'Should you take one now? I'm not going to stop every two minutes for you to throw up.'

Sadie ignored his warning. Stopping every two minutes didn't exactly sound like a picnic to her either. 'I'll wait till we get out of the city. Save my performance for the windy bits.'

Kent narrowed his eyes as he took the opportunity to study her face some more. She had dark rings surrounding the deep grey of her irises, which seemed to lure him in even further. 'Just how trippy is trippy?'

Sadie realised his mouth was quite near and she had to wonder what it would look like kicked up a little, those creases becoming deep grooves, because it looked pretty damn perfect as it was. As if some old master with an eye for masculine perfection had sculpted it just for him, and the artist in her, never far from the surface, appreciated its flawlessness.

The woman, on the other hand, was just plain jealous.

Her own ridiculously plump mouth, devoid of collagen despite what every catty woman she'd ever met had implied, seemed garish by comparison. It was why she rarely wore lipstick or gloss.

Her mouth did not need any more attention.

Kent felt her gaze on his mouth and the pull of those incredible eyes as she studied him. 'Sadie?' he prompted.

Sadie blinked as she realised he was frowning and she was staring. Not only that, but she'd lost her place in the conversation. Her brain scrambled to catch up. She took a step back from him. What *had* they been talking about?

Pills. Right. 'I sing,' she said. 'Loudly. And not very well.'

Kent grimaced. Great. Stuck in a car with karaoke Barbie. 'Try to refrain.' He looked at his watch and said, 'Let's go.'

Sadie took a deep breath as she headed to the passenger seat. Her heart thudded in her chest on a surge of adrenaline. The call of the wild? The excitement of a new adventure? The beginnings of an illustrious career?

She hoped so because the alternatives weren't palatable. Dread at the oncoming nausea. Or, worse, being alone in a confined space with an unimpressed man whose mouth had her wishing she'd paid more attention in sculpting classes.

She'd climbed up into the high-clearance, all-wheel drive. At five eight, she wasn't exactly short, but Sadie still felt as if pole-vaulting lessons would have been handy. The sturdy cab felt like a cocoon of armour around her, even if the ground seemed a long way down.

As soon as she buckled up Kent thrust a folded up map at her. 'Here,' he said. 'I've marked the journey in red.'

Sadie looked at him as the mere thought of having to *read* and travel made her feel ill. 'You don't have a GPS?'

Kent shot her an impatient look. 'We're doing this the old-fashioned way,' he said and started the engine.

Fabulous. 'And what happens if we lose the map?' she enquired sweetly. 'Do we use the stars?'

Kent suppressed a smile at her derision. He held her gaze. 'Unfortunately I didn't bring my sextant.'

That look—intense, focused—fanned over her like a sticky web, doing strange things to her pulse and causing heat to bloom in her belly and other places further south.

Oh, he'd brought his sextant all right…

CHAPTER TWO

EVEN though she was looking out of the window, Sadie didn't notice the city streets of Sydney giving way to the red rooves of suburbia or to the greenery of semi-rural market gardens. She was too busy puzzling over her reaction to the man sitting an arm's length away.

On the surface, he was everything she didn't usually go for. Physically impressive. Outdoorsy. A beer and football kind of a guy.

But then there was his age.

Through some online investigation last night she'd discovered he was thirty-six and she *did* have a track record with older men.

Leo had been twenty years her senior.

She supposed a psychologist would say she had a Daddy Complex. Her father had left when she was twelve and got himself a new family, including a set of twins who'd turned into sports-mad little boys.

She'd always felt the fact that she was a girl and had been more arty than sporty had been a huge let-down for her father. And after years of trying to win his attention and affection she'd finally conceded defeat as she'd headed off to college.

So, maybe his abandonment *had* spread invisible tentacles into her life.

Whatever.

It didn't change the facts. Nothing else about Kent Nelson should have appealed.

Yet somehow it did.

She studied his profile as he drove, his eyes fixed on the road. His buzz cut melded into the stubble of his sideburns, which flowed into that covering his jaw, hugging the spare planes of his face, emphasising cheekbones that stood out like railings. It made him look…severe. A far cry from the bearded guy who had been laughing at the camera in the snap from the gallery.

It made him look intense.

Guarded.

It made him look haunted.

As a journalist, and a huge fan of his work, it was exceedingly intriguing.

As a woman—it scared the hell out of her.

Kent gripped the steering wheel as Sadie's speculative gaze seemed to burn a hole at the angle of his jaw. After almost eighteen months in and out of hospitals and another six months of physical therapy, it had been a while since he'd had any kind of constant company—female or otherwise—and her concentration was unnerving.

He turned to look at her and almost rolled his eyes as she quickly pretended she hadn't been staring at him by feigning interest in the scenery outside her window.

Very mature.

His gaze fell to her legs, the denim riding well and truly up above her knees and pulling taut across thighs as lush and round as the rest of her. *Rubenesque* slipped into his brain and he flicked his gaze back to the road.

'I hope you brought something warmer—it's going to get cold out at night.'

Sadie blinked. They'd been in the car for over an hour

and this was the first thing he said to her? She really, really hoped he wasn't one of those men who thought there was a direct correlation between her cup size and her IQ.

She slapped her forehead theatrically. 'And I only packed bikinis and a frilly negligee.'

Kent gripped the steering wheel as images of her in a bikini screwed with his concentration. 'A lot of people think of the outback as hot,' he quantified, still not looking at her. 'But it cools down really quickly at night.'

Sadie shot him an impatient look. 'Thank you. But how about we assume from now on I'm a reasonably intelligent person who wouldn't go on any trip without having thoroughly researched it first?'

Kent turned his head at the note in her voice. It was more than sarcasm. It was…touchy. As if she'd had to prove her intelligence one too many times. He guessed with her assets people didn't often see beyond them.

He looked back at the road. 'Fair enough.'

Sadie groaned as they passed a sign indicating their ascent through the Blue Mountains was about to begin. It came with a warning of sharp corners and hairpin bends.

The nausea kicked in at the thought of what lay ahead. '*Fabulous*,' she muttered as she searched through her bag for her pills. 'Dangerous curves.'

Kent wished there were a pill he could take for the ones inside the car, but her look of abject misery kept his brain off her treacherous curves. He could practically hear her teeth grinding as she pawed through the contents of a handbag big enough to fit an entire pharmacy full of motion sickness tablets.

For crying out loud! 'Do you get sick if you're the driver?' he asked.

Sadie shook her head absently, missing the exasperation in his tone as she read the back of the medication box.

It was a new brand to her, one supposedly with reduced side effects. 'Nope.'

'Well, that's easy, then, isn't it?' he said as he indicated and pulled the car into one of the regular truck laybys that lined the route.

'What are you doing?' Sadie frowned as he unbuckled.

'Letting you drive.'

Sadie didn't move for a moment. 'You want me to drive your car?'

He nodded. 'You do have a licence, right?'

Sadie looked around at the behemoth in which she was sitting. She drove a second-hand Prius. 'Not a tank licence.'

Kent's mouth pressed into an impatient line. 'You'll be fine.' He stepped out and strode around to her side.

Sadie had the ridiculous urge to lock her door before he reached her, but then it was open and he was filling the space along with the whoosh of traffic and the acrid aroma of exhaust fumes.

She looked at Kent, surprised at her elevated height to find she was looking him straight in the eye. They were brown, she noticed, now she was focused on something other than his mouth. She was close enough to see flecks of copper and amber shimmering there too, throwing a hue into the darker brown. They reminded her of something—a memory—she couldn't quite recall.

Kent watched her watching him as if she was trying to figure something out. 'Don't they say an ounce of prevention is worth a pound of cure?' he prompted.

Sadie suddenly remembered. The tiger-eye marble she'd had in her collection as a kid. One of her father's many attempts to get her interested in something other than reading and drawing.

'Are you sure?' she asked, looking around the vehicle

again, absently pulling her bottom lip between her teeth. If it had been a hire car she wouldn't have hesitated. 'I've never driven anything quite so...big. I'd hate to crash it.'

Kent did not drop his gaze to her mouth. The fact that he even noticed her lip being ravished by her teeth was irritating enough. He raised an eyebrow. 'Do you make a habit of crashing cars?'

She shook her head, releasing her lip. 'No, never.' She looked back at him and frowned. She'd have thought a he-man like Kent would never have relinquished the wheel.

'What?' he asked warily.

Sadie shook her head. 'I've never met a man yet who'd give up the driver's seat for a woman.' Her father had never let her mother drive when they were in the car together. 'Doesn't it emasculate you or something?'

Kent blinked. That hadn't been a question he'd expected. What kind of Neanderthals did she hang out with? 'I think I'm secure enough in my masculinity to not be threatened by a woman in the driver's seat.'

Sadie's gaze dropped from the spiky stubble of his angular jaw to the breadth of his shoulders. She had to admit if this man's masculinity could be threatened then no man's was safe!

'Look,' he said impatiently as she continued to sit. 'It's win-win. You don't get to throw up every two minutes and I get to spot photo opps. I also don't get to see you all trippy, which, given that we hardly know each other, is a good thing.'

Sadie couldn't dispute his logic. The last thing she needed was to lose her inhibitions around a man who looked as if he kept his well and truly in check.

If he had any.

'Fine.'

Sadie undid her belt and twisted in her seat to get out.

She glanced at him, waiting for him to shift, her gaze snagging on his mouth. He didn't for a moment and there was a split second when neither of them moved. When his beautiful mouth filled her entire vision and she found herself wishing he would say something just so she could admire how it moved. Then he stepped back and she half slid, half jumped to the ground on legs that seemed suddenly wobbly.

After giving Sadie a quick tutorial on the various idiosyncrasies of his vehicle, Kent left her to it, making no comment as she lurched it out onto the highway. Her grip on the steering wheel was turning her knuckles white and he was afraid she might split all the skin there if she didn't ease up.

'Relax,' he ordered. 'You're doing fine.'

Strangely his command did not help Sadie relax. Her gaze flicked between the rear view and side mirrors as her heartbeat pelted along in time to the engine. She wasn't sure if it was from nervousness about driving a strange car/tank that belonged to someone else or the weird moment she and Kent had shared as she'd exited the vehicle.

'Relax,' he said again.

'Believe it or not,' Sadie said, gritting her teeth as she eyeballed the road, 'you telling me to relax is *not* helping.'

Kent held up his hands in surrender. 'Okay.'

'I just need to get used it,' she quantified. 'It's not normal to be so high up. I feel like I'm driving a truck.'

Kent grimaced. It was hardly a semi-trailer. 'I said okay.'

He turned then and dragged his camera case out of the back passenger floor well. Sadie was obviously stressed about driving the big, bad vehicle and he had little patience with princesses. Best to keep himself occupied and his lip zipped. And one more equipment check before they got too far away from civilisation wouldn't go astray.

About ten minutes later he noticed her grip slacken and her shoulders relax back into the seat. Ten minutes after that she even started multitasking.

'So. What's the plan?' Sadie asked, more comfortable now with how the car handled. 'Where are our scheduled stops?'

Kent looked up from his disassembled camera. 'Scheduled stops?'

Sadie nodded. 'You know? Of a night time? When we're tired?'

'I hadn't scheduled any stops. We're driving all the way through.'

Sadie looked briefly away from the road to blast him with a *you-have-to-be-kidding me* look. A non-stop journey would probably take two full days.

Without a single break?

'Don't we have to sleep some time?'

He speared her with a direct look. 'Do you really want to make this journey any longer than it has to be? We can pull over and catch some kip along the way. Either in the car or I have a couple of swags.'

Sadie supressed a shudder. *Oh, goody. Maybe they'd find a jolly jumbuck to stuff inside.* She flicked a quick glance towards him. 'I don't camp.'

Kent blinked at the way she said camp—as if she'd said prison. 'What do you mean, you don't camp?'

'It's simple,' she said, returning her eyes to the road. 'You don't fly. I don't camp.'

Great. Car sick. Didn't camp. Sadie Bliss was stacking up the black marks against her name and truly pushing his patience. 'What on earth have you got against sleeping under the stars?'

'Nothing,' Sadie assured him. 'Give me five of them and I'm happy as a pig in mud.'

Kent shook his head. 'You haven't lived, city girl.'

'I guess we're just going to have to agree to disagree on that one,' she said sweetly.

Kent's mouth took on a grim line. 'I have a feeling there may be a bit of that this trip.'

Sadie did too. 'So? Where should we stop tonight, do you think?' she prompted.

Kent pulled the map out of the glovebox, where Sadie had thrown it in disgust earlier, and did some calculations. 'It's about another ten hours to Cunnamulla,' he said, looking at the digital clock display on the dash. It was just gone nine-thirty. 'That'll put us there after seven tonight. It'll also put us over the Queensland border.'

'Okay.' Sadie nodded.

'Doubt there's any five-star accommodation there though,' he mused. 'We could go another couple hours on to Charleville. It's twice the size. Still don't think they run to five star.'

Sadie shot him a sarcastic smile. 'Thanks, I'll settle for a shower, a flushing toilet and a bed.'

'Cunnamulla it is.'

With that sorted, silence reigned as they wended their way through the beautiful Blue Mountains, and down the other side of the Great Dividing Range. Kent went back to his camera bag, soothed by the familiarity of the routine. It had been a while since he'd lugged this stuff around, lived with it every day, and it was comforting to know it still felt good.

He occasionally shot a glance Sadie's way. He had to admit, after her initial misgivings she was handling the vehicle with great competence. He'd been afraid she was going to whine about the heavy steering or the engine noise or the lack of a stereo system all the way to Borroloola, but she'd got on with the job with no complaints.

No chatter whatsoever.

His kind of travelling companion.

Until it all went to hell two minutes later.

'So are we going to sit in silence or are we going to get to know each other?' she asked.

Now she was out of the worst of the windy roads Sadie was free to concentrate on other things. And it had occurred to her that she was sitting next to a man who was pretty hot property, especially since he'd gone underground. How far would a feature on *the* Kent Nelson get her career? If she had to spend days on end in a car with his particular brand of he-man, she might as well get something for it.

And truly, the way he kept breaking down that camera and reassembling it, as if it were a gun, was slightly unnerving.

Kent sighed. He should have known it was too good to be true. 'Silence is golden.'

Sadie quirked an eyebrow at his terse reply. 'Silence is loud.'

He clicked a lens in place, then looked at her. 'Listen to me, Sadie Bliss. Let's not pretend that either of us is too thrilled by being stuck in this car together. I know women feel the need to chat and fill up all the empty spaces, but I'm okay with the empty spaces.' It sure as hell beat the crowding in his head. 'I like the empty spaces.'

'I don't feel the need,' she dismissed irritably. 'It's just, you know…conversational. Polite.'

Kent shoved the camera back in its soft-sided bag. 'I can handle rude.'

That she could believe. But she doubted she could. 'So…

we're just going to…not talk? For three thousand kilometres?'

'Well, I'm sure we'll need to say the odd word or two. Like, "*We need petrol*," and, "*How about here for lunch*?" But let's try and keep it to a minimum, huh?'

Sadie blinked at his hard profile. His arrogance that she'd just fall in with his imperious command irked. He might be used to women falling over themselves to do as he said, but she just wasn't built that way.

And his insistence on silence only piqued her curiosity. The shadows in his eyes told her there was stuff he didn't want to talk about. And she was pretty sure his refusal to fly was just scratching the surface. Just looking at his guarded exterior made her want to know more.

She wanted to ask about the picture. She wanted to know about that day.

Probably best not to start there though…

She waited a few minutes to lull him into a false sense of security. They were heading for Mudgee on a relatively straight stretch of highway, the scenery fairly standard Australian bush fare. Lots of gums and low, scrubby vegetation.

Fairly uninspiring really.

Especially compared to the story she knew he must be harbouring deep down where the shadows lived.

He'd just opened the map when she said, 'It could be fun.' She waited a beat. 'Getting to know each other.'

Kent didn't look up from the map. 'I doubt it.'

He already knew too much about her. Curves that wouldn't quit. A mouth that was made to be kissed. A weak constitution and a penchant for five-star living.

Trouble.

A real pain in his butt.

Sadie took his blunt rejection on the chin and was

pleased she didn't insult easily. Nor did she dissuade. 'Oh, come on,' Sadie goaded. 'It's really easy when you try. See, I ask something about you. We discuss it. Then you ask something about me.'

He kept his nose in the map and Sadie felt a peculiar desperation. Why, she wasn't sure.

'Easy,' she added as the silence built.

It built some more.

'Oh, come on, there must be something you want to know about me.'

Kent looked up at her, regarding her steadily. She'd obviously been to the terrier school of journalism.

Excellent. Chatty and dogged.

Two more black marks.

He suddenly remembered wondering yesterday why Leonard Pinto had requested a rookie journo for his feature.

'Why did Leonard Pinto want you?'

Sadie almost choked on her own spit as the question caught her unawares. She certainly hadn't been prepared for his first question to skip so much of the preliminary stuff that was the norm in these situations. Where were you born? How old are you? Where'd you go to school?

Or even the ruder ones that people tended to just come straight out and ask her no matter how inappropriate.

Is that your real name?

Are those your real boobs?

Do you have silicone in those lips?

'Jeez,' she said lightly, letting her sarcastic nature run free. 'Cutting straight to the chase. No name, rank and serial number? No opening pleasantries? I hope you're more subtle than this on dates.'

Kent raised his eyebrows at her deliberate sidestep, but

he hadn't missed the whitening of her knuckles on the steering wheel.

'I'm rusty.'

Sadie snorted. The man looked utterly well oiled. In one hundred per cent working order. Even his limp didn't seem to impede him. 'You don't say?'

Kent watched her for a moment or two as she kept her gaze firmly on the road ahead. Her profile was as striking as the rest of her, from her wavy hair to her pouty lips to the thrust of her breasts.

And he really, really didn't want to be noticing her breasts. 'Why does Pinto want you?' he repeated.

Sadie flicked a quick glance his way. 'Why don't you fly?'

Kent blinked. He hadn't expected her to push back so quickly. Or for her salvo to hit its target quite so effectively. 'Is he a relative?' he persisted.

Sadie didn't even let a beat go by. 'Is it because of the chopper accident?' she replied.

Kent narrowed his gaze as he looked at her and she turned and shot him a *two-can-play-at-this-game* look before returning her attention to the road. 'Or maybe he saw your picture on the magazine website and just wants to get into your pants?' he parried.

It might only be a head shot, but a man who painted nudes for a living had to appreciate the perfect pout of that mouth.

The air in Sadie's lungs stuttered to a halt as she forgot to breathe in for a few seconds. Her fingers tightened on the steering wheel. She wasn't about to tell him that Leonard Pinto had been in her pants plenty.

And that there was no way he'd want to go there again. Not with her carrying so much weight.

'You're right,' she said, slamming the car into a lower gear as she slowed for some roadworks. 'Silence *is* golden.'

Kent shot her a sardonic smile. 'I knew you'd see it my way.'

Half an hour later Sadie was pretty bored with the scenery. Kent had the buds of his MP3 player in his ears and was intermittently flipping through a travel book or gazing out at the scenery flashing by. Occasionally she could see those fascinating lips moving—presumably to the music she couldn't hear.

Or he hadn't taken his meds today.

He sure hadn't taken his chatty pill.

He seemed to be having a little party for one in his seat—perfectly content—and it irritated her. If he seriously thought he could ignore her for three thousand kilometres, then he truly did need those meds.

It should have been refreshing to be ignored by a man for a change. But it was strangely off-putting. Attention she could deal with. She could deflect. But inattention, lack of interest even, that wasn't in her repertoire.

She was going to get him talking if it killed her.

She reached across and yanked on the closest ear bud. 'How about a game, instead?' she suggested as he fixed her with a steady glare.

Kent waited a beat of two before replying. *She wanted to play games?* He notched up another black mark as he held out his hand for the bud. 'No.'

'Come on,' she cajoled undeterred. 'This is supposed to be a road trip, right? You play games on road trips. It's in all the movies.'

Kent refused to think about the kind of games he could play with Sadie Bliss. He was not going to think about strip anything. He wasn't going there. 'I don't do games,' he said bluntly as he relieved her of his ear bud.

She quirked an eyebrow. 'What, not even I Spy?'

Kent regarded her for a moment, all perky and pushy. He needed to nip that in the bud or this trip was going to be interminable. 'How about truth or dare?'

Sadie's pulse spiked at the silky note in his voice and the way his gaze seemed to flick, ever so briefly, to her mouth. It was tempting but she doubted he'd go for truth. And she was damned if she was going to dare this man to do anything.

'Maybe once we've got to know each other a little better?' she retreated.

Kent pulled his gaze away from her, startled at the thought. He didn't want to know Sadie Bliss. A sign flashed by and he grabbed a mental hold. 'I spy with my little eye,' he said, 'something beginning with petrol station.'

Sadie kept her eyes firmly on the indicated services ahead. She scrunched her brow. 'You know you're only supposed to say the first letter, right?'

He ignored her sarcasm. 'Pull in, I'm starving. Breakfast seems a very long time ago.'

Sadie had been starving for the last three days. 'We've only been in the car for three hours,' she pointed out.

'I need snacks,' he said. 'And you can use the facilities.'

'Gee, thanks,' Sadie said rolling her eyes as she indicated left. 'But my days of enforced toileting ended a long, long time ago. You may have women in your life with weak bladders but, I can assure you, mine is made of cast iron.'

'So it's just your stomach that's weak?' he enquired drily.

Sadie shot him a look as she prepared to park. 'Really?

You want to annoy me now? As I'm parking *your* tank in this itty-bitty car space?'

Kent assessed the one remaining, very narrow car space. She made a good point. 'Nope.'

Sadie turned back to the job at hand as she nervously pulled the car into the middle of three parking bays. The heavy steering was fine for wide open spaces but it felt as if she was trying to grapple a huge metallic beast into a matchbox as she centred the vehicle.

It was gratifying to get a grunt of respect from Kent.

He flung his door open as soon as she killed the engine. 'You coming?'

Sadie shook her head. 'I'm good.'

'You want something?'

She shook it again. 'I brought some snacks with me.'

Sadie watched him stride to the sliding doors of the service station, pleased to be released from his company for a few minutes. His jeans gently hugged his bottom and the backs of his thighs without being skin tight. His T-shirt was loose enough for the breeze to blow it against the broad contours of his back. And his limp, barely discernible, added an extra edge to his rugged appeal.

A blonde woman with a baby on her hip coming out of the sliding door as Kent went in actually stood for a moment admiring the view. She seemed perplexed for a second after the closing glass doors snatched him away. As if she couldn't remember why she was standing in the car park gawping at a closed door.

I hear ya, honey.

He was back in a few minutes loaded down with enough carbohydrates to exceed his recommended daily intake from now until the end of his days. She felt hyperglycaemic just looking at them.

'Here,' he said as he passed her a packet of Twisties. 'I got one for you, too.'

Twisties? Dear God, he was going to eat Twisties—her one weakness—right in front of her. She passed them back.

'Thanks, I've got these,' she said, waving a celery stick at him.

Kent grimaced as he opened his packet. 'You're going to eat *celery*? On a road trip.'

He had a way of emphasising celery as if it were suet or tripe. 'It's healthy,' she said defensively, and was about to launch into a spiel about the amazing properties of the wonder food when the aroma of carbohydrates wafted out to greet her like an old friend and she momentarily lost her train of thought.

How could that special blend of additives and preservatives smell so damn good? Her stomach growled.

Loudly.

Kent raised an eyebrow. 'I think your stomach wants a say.'

Sadie stuffed the celery into her mouth and started the car to stop her from reaching over and lifting a lurid orange piece out and devouring it like the Cookie Monster. 'It's because I listen to my stomach too damn often that I'm as big as I am,' she muttered testily as she reversed.

Kent eyed her critically as he buckled up, thinking she looked pretty damn good to him. He shook his head. Women in the western world amazed him. Their lives were so privileged they had nothing but trivialities to worry about. He really didn't have the patience for it.

'Please tell me you're not going to eat celery for three days.'

Sadie gave him an exasperated glare. 'What's it matter to you?'

He bugged his eyes at her. To think less than two years

ago he had been in the thick of a combat zone and now he was talking to a madwoman with a weak constitution but an apparently strong bladder about *celery* of all things.

'I think it's making you cranky.'

Sadie flicked her gaze to the road, then back at him. He had orange Twistie dust on the tips of his fingers and his lips, which just went to show perfection could be improved upon. She wondered what he'd taste like beneath the flavours of salt and cheese.

Her stomach growled again and she started to salivate.

And not for celery.

Maybe not even for Twisties.

'No,' she denied, looking back to the road. 'You and your damn Twisties are making me cranky.'

'I guess that means you won't want any M&M's either?' he enquired.

Sadie almost groaned out loud. How on earth did he keep in such magnificent shape? She could feel the fat cells on her butt multiplying just by looking at the familiar chocolate snacks.

'Thank you,' she denied primly. 'I'll stick with my celery.'

Kent shrugged. 'Suit yourself,' he said as he threw a Twistie into the air near his face and caught it in his mouth.

The crunch thankfully drowned out another resounding growl from her belly.

By the time they'd crossed the state border and arrived in Cunnamulla, Sadie was definitely ready to call it a day. She was tired and over her strong, silent travelling companion, who had snacked all day, read, slept, listened to music and devoured two pies and a large carton of iced-coffee for lunch, whilst disparaging her pumpkin and feta salad with a Diet Coke.

All with only the barest minimum of conversation.

She wanted a shower. Then a bed.

The welcome glow of a vacancy sign cheered her enormously. 'This okay?' she asked him.

Kent nodded. 'As good as any, I guess.'

Sadie parked the car in front of the reception and she and Kent went inside, the night air already starting to cool.

'Two rooms, please,' Sadie said to the middle-aged woman behind the desk.

'I'm sorry, we only have one left,' she apologised.

'Oh,' Sadie murmured, her shoulders sagging.

The woman looked from Sadie to Kent, then back to Sadie, and brightened. 'It has two doubles, though?'

Kent opened his mouth to tell the woman they'd go elsewhere but Sadie, standing tall again, butted in. 'We'll take it.'

He blinked at her. 'I'm sure there are other hotels here that will have two separate rooms,' he said to her.

'I'm sure there are,' Sadie agreed wearily. 'And if you want to go and track them down I'll wish you luck. But I'm exhausted. My butt is numb. The thought of getting back in the car again makes me want to cry. So I'm going to stay right here, if it's all the same to you.'

Kent looked down at her doe eyes, the lashes fluttering against her cheek. She did look pretty done in and she had driven all day without complaint.

'Fine. I can sleep in the car.'

Sadie cocked an eyebrow. She doubted the confines of his back car seat would be very accommodating for a man of his proportions. 'I'm an adult. You're an adult. There are two beds. I promise not to wake up in the middle of the night and try to seduce you.'

Kent gave her a grudging smile. His first for the day.

'Well, now you've just taken all the fun out of it. And you, going to the trouble of bringing your frilly negligee.'

Sadie blinked, surprised to discover that beneath all that guarded silence, a sense of humour lurked. 'Well, will you look at that,' she murmured. 'He does know how to smile.'

Kent suppressed another smile. 'Don't get used to it.'

Sadie absently massaged her neck, too tired for this conversation. 'Fine, tough guy, sleep in the car. Just don't moan tomorrow when you have a crick in your neck.'

He shrugged. 'I've slept far rougher.' Being embedded with active forces in the Middle East on several occasions had been far from luxurious.

Not that he'd slept much then.

Or now, for that matter.

Sadie sighed. 'Well, bully for you, He-man.'

Kent was so surprised by the nickname he actually laughed this time. He'd never been called that before, at least not to his face, and it was bemusing. 'Did you just call me a he-man?'

Sadie felt his laughter undulate through every muscle in her body right down to her toes. It might have taken her all day but it had been worth the wait. 'I call it as I see it.'

Kent opened his mouth to deny it but Sadie was looking up at him with long, sleepy blinks and he had the wildest urge to see what she'd look like between motel sheets.

He turned to the woman behind the desk, who'd been watching their exchange like an engrossed spectator at a tennis match. 'Where do I sign?' he asked.

CHAPTER THREE

THE room was clean but basic. A bar fridge, a television, a bathroom. And two very hard-looking double beds. Still, they beckoned, more inviting than a Bedouin tent, and right now Sadie wouldn't have swapped it for the Waldorf Astoria.

'I bags the shower,' she said as she threw her backpack on the bed closest to the bathroom and delved through it for some clean clothes.

'Do you want something to eat?' Kent asked plonking himself on the other bed and flipping through the information folder placed next to the fluffy towel folded into a fan with a wrapped bar of soap strategically placed in the centre. 'They serve bar meals until eight.'

Sadie was starving. But not as much as she was sleepy. She was used to denying herself food. Sleep not so much. Sleep was as vital to her as air.

And woe betide anyone who deprived her.

'Nope,' she said, picking up her towel.

'Celery again?' Kent asked.

He wasn't sure how much she'd brought in that fridge bag but there seemed to be an endless supply of it today. Every time he opened a packet of something or rustled a wrapper more appeared.

Sadie was too exhausted to make a pithy comeback.

'Too tired. Need to sleep,' she muttered, closing the bathroom door even before the last word was out of her mouth.

Kent heard the shower turn on and fell back against the bed. It felt like a rock and he literally bounced a little. The back seat of his vehicle would have been softer. But then it wouldn't have had a hot, busty, naked woman just three metres and a wall away.

Getting wet. Getting soapy.

He felt heat bloom in his loins and placed the open information folder over his face.

Sadie Bliss was a bad idea. No matter what her body, her delectable smart mouth, her quick wit or her name might suggest.

He didn't need a psych consult to know he was still pretty messed up. He'd had nearly two years of being held ransom by his body and the surgeons and physios had pronounced him cured—or as cured as he was going to get. But it was pretty dark inside his head still. He'd put off tackling the psychological fallout from the accident, thinking and hoping that time would heal as it had his physical ailments.

But it hadn't.

So, he really didn't need a fling with Sadie Bliss. Or, more importantly, she didn't need a fling with him.

He wasn't in a good headspace.

And she was too chatty, too pushy.

Too young.

He didn't have a right to screw with that.

What he needed to do was get back to what he was good at—taking pictures. Use his art as therapy. As a way back to the rest of his life. Then he could worry about the Sadie Blisses of the world.

He heard the taps shut off.

Pictured her reaching for her towel...

He sat up and pulled his shirt off. The room was stuffy and he suddenly felt very hot. He wondered over to the air-con panel and flicked it on. Then he picked up the phone on his bedside table and placed an order with the woman at the desk. He prowled to the bar fridge, pulled out a bottle of beer, parked his butt against the cabinet, cracked the lid and took a fortifying gulp.

The harsh metallic rattle from the shower curtain being pulled back rang like chimes of doom around the room.

Lord. Just how thin were these walls?

And then came a blood-curdling scream.

Sadie had never seen a spider so huge in all her life. She saw the odd tiny creature scurrying around her flat but she was pretty adept at wielding a can of insect spray, and it seemed the local population of creepy crawlies had put the word out to avoid Sadie's abode at all costs.

But this thing, hanging on the back of the door as if it were the mother ship, was a monster. It was big, and hairy and very, very ugly.

There was a belting on the door followed by, 'Sadie!'

The spider didn't even move at the noise so near its epicentre—yes, it was big enough to have an epicentre—and nor did Sadie. 'Kent!'

'Are you okay?' he demanded through the door.

'Big, big, *big* spider,' she called.

Kent looked at the door in disbelief. A *spider*? Her horror-flick scream had scared ten years off his life. Did she have a clue how very trivial a spider was in the grand scheme of things?

Now, some of the things he'd seen—they were worth screaming about.

'Bloody hell Sadie, I thought you were being murdered.'

'If this thing gets hold of me, I'm sure it'll have a good go,' she yelled.

'It can't be that big.'

'It is,' she said, anchoring the towel more securely under her arm.

And it was between her and her clothes.

She eyed her pyjamas hanging on the back of the door. Had the spider crawled over them? She shuddered at the thought.

Just how long had it been in here watching her?

'I think it's one of those bird eating suckers,' she announced.

'The ones that are only found in South America?'

Sadie shook her head. 'Not any more.'

'Sadie…'

'Okay, I know, I'm sorry. I'm a horrible girly, city-chick cliché. But truly it's huge and spiders just plain creep me out.'

Kent leaned his forehead against the door. He'd been landed with a car-sick, celery-eating, arachnophobe.

Who'd have thought that would come in such a fine package?

'What do you want me to do?'

Even through the door Sadie could hear his exasperation. Could sense his impatience with her girly theatrics. But it was easy to judge when you were on the other side of the door—*the safe side*. 'I want you to come in here and kill it!'

Kent sighed. The fact that she was being held captive in the bathroom by a spider didn't bother him a bit—eventually she'd have to figure it out herself. And if he only had faith she'd do it silently he'd leave her to it.

But a day in a car with Sadie Bliss had told him she didn't really do quiet contemplation. 'Are you decent?'

Sadie rolled her eyes. 'Why? Do you think the spider cares?' she yelled.

He took a breath. 'I'm coming in.'

'Easy, very easy,' Sadie ordered. 'It's on the back of the door and I do not want to see how far that thing can jump.'

Kent opened the door slowly whilst Sadie watched his progress, her eyes peeking out over the edge of the shower curtain she'd pulled around herself for extra protection as if it were an invisibility cloak.

Kent glanced her way, two doe eyes and the top of her head the only things visible as she eyeballed the back of the door. 'You know it's more scared of you than you are of it, right?' he murmured as he slowly opened the door further.

Sadie didn't take her eyes off the terrifying arachnid. 'I doubt it.' It looked like something from an ancient Roman arena.

Once the door was almost all the way open and Sadie could no longer see the hairy critter she relaxed slightly. She looked at Kent, realising for the first time he was shirt-less. His broad chest and flat abdomen, complete with a light smattering of hair that arrowed down behind the band of his low-slung jeans, filled her vision.

It was truly a sight to behold.

Why was it again she'd never been into buff men?

For a moment she almost forgot she was being terrorised by a mutant spider.

Almost.

'Right,' she whispered, dragging her gaze off his chest to the other terrifying object in the room. 'I'm going to climb out of the bath and walk very slowly towards you. Once I'm safely out of the room you can do your he-man thing.'

Kent wasn't entirely sure he was ready for Sadie to come out from behind the curtain. But he sure as hell wanted to see the creature that had Little-Miss-Curves all het up.

'Okay,' he whispered dramatically back, her dirty look bouncing easily off his shoulders.

Sadie quietly pushed back the curtain and gingerly stepped out of the bath. She could feel Kent's gaze on her and couldn't figure out which animal to keep her eye on the most.

She gripped the towel more firmly to her body.

Slowly she sidled along the wall furthest from the door, edged around the vanity basin where her toiletry bag sat. When she drew level with Kent she realised they were just one hotel towel and a pair of Levi's from being naked. His bare, broad shoulders and his spare stubbled face filled her vision. He smelled of Twisties and beer.

Who'd have ever thought *that could* be such a potent combination?

'Thank you,' she murmured as he fell back against the front of the door to allow her to squeeze past.

And it was a squeeze. Her body brushed his as she slipped from the room and Kent felt the caress of towelling against his chest all the way down to his groin. For a moment he stood still and did nothing; the impact of her eyes, her mouth, her bare creamy shoulders and the damp tendrils of hair framing it all was temporarily paralysing.

But he was aware of her watching him, her hands fidgeting while she waited for his *he-man* move, and his brain came back online.

He strode into the bathroom and slowly shut the door. Her clothes were hanging on the back. And, yes, he had to admit, it was one of the larger Huntsman spiders he'd seen. He shook his head and grabbed her clothes. The spider scuttled to the top of the door, then onto the ceiling. He walked over to the bath/shower unit, stepped into the tub to open the window on the wall opposite the shower head so the poor creature could make its escape.

He turned to step out, his gaze falling on a scrap of material hanging on the shower-curtain rail. A silky-looking pink thong with a little diamanté twinkling at the front.

For a heartbeat there was nothing in his head but elevator music. Then there was a whole lot more.

None of it conducive to his sanity.

None of it conducive to going out there and facing her again.

'Is it gone?'

Her voice sliced like a machete through the inappropriate images in his head and Kent dragged his transfixed gaze off Sadie's underwear to the back of the door. He stepped out of the tub and had the door open in two strides.

'Not yet,' he said, thrusting her clothes at her and shutting the door behind him. 'I opened the window. It'll crawl out soon enough.'

Sadie blinked. 'You did what?' She clutched her clothes to her chest. 'Are you nuts? You opened the window? So all his mates could join him?' She took a step back. 'What if it doesn't go?'

It was the second time she'd questioned his mental faculties and, even if they weren't already a little on the dicey side, her silky pink thong probably hadn't helped. He wished she'd get dressed already. Damp strands of dark hair brushed creamy shoulders offsetting the natural rouge of her mouth and, frankly, insane had never looked so damn good.

Kent smiled patiently. 'We'll keep the door shut.'

'What if it crawls back in here, under the door? What if it runs over my face in the middle of the night?' She shuddered. 'You do know human beings are supposed to swallow eight spiders in their lifetime, right?'

He clamped down on the urge to tell her there was no way she'd choke that sucker down and instead rolled his eyes. 'I'm sure it's looking for the fastest exit it can make, Sadie. It's probably just trying to recover from the stroke it suffered when you screamed fit to wake the dead. I'm surprised the cops haven't been called to investigate.'

Sadie shook her head mutinously. 'I need it dead. I won't be able to sleep knowing its alive and in here. And trust me, you *do not* want to be around me when I'm sleep deprived.'

'Because you're such a treat now?'

'Please,' she asked. 'Please get rid of it.'

Kent knew he was doomed. He would have done just about anything that mouth was asking. Hell, he would have slain a dragon for her had there been one of those in the bathroom.

'Fine.'

He stalked to his bed and unzipped a long side pocket of his backpack, pulling out a metal walking cane he'd brought along in case there was some serious hiking required to find the perfect shot. He adjusted its length, then returned to the bathroom, ignoring Sadie, who was watching the shut door with trepidation.

He kicked the door shut behind him to block out the view of her still-naked-beneath-the-towel stance, only to have her push it open again. 'Oh, no, you don't,' she said from behind him. 'I want to see it dead. I don't want you coming back out here telling me it's gone just to shut me up because you think I'm being neurotic.'

Kent turned. She was standing back a little from the doorway, her large grey eyes piercing him with a do-not-mess-with-me look.

Kent raised an eyebrow. 'I see we have trust issues.'

Sadie glared at him. 'My issues are none of your damn business. Just make it dead.'

Kent grinned at her prickliness as he turned back to locate the poor creature who'd had the supreme bad luck of choosing this particular room to explore. Although, seeing a naked Sadie Bliss had to have been some consolation.

It was crouched in the corner of the ceiling above the bath. 'Come on, itsy-bitsy,' he said as he approached the bath, the walking stick extended. 'Time to move along.'

Sadie inched a little closer. 'I said dead, damn it,' she snapped from the doorway

'Yeh, yeh, don't get your knickers in a twist,' he said as he positioned himself.

Bad. Word. Choice.

The diamanté from Sadie's thong glimmered in the light and tantalised his peripheral vision.

Sadie's gaze was drawn to it too. *Oh, no!* She hadn't meant to leave it hanging there. She'd just forgotten everything the second *itsy-bitsy* decided to show.

What the hell must he be thinking?

'Right,' Kent said, pushing the rounded knob of the stick towards the spider. 'Time to move along.'

'What are you doing?' she snapped again.

'I'm not killing the spider, Sadie,' he said as he gently swept it towards the open window.

Sadie gasped as the spider scuttled onto the end of the stick. She took a step back as she opened her mouth to warn Kent but in two seconds he'd dropped the stick from vertical to horizontal, the end with the spider poking out of the window. Once it hit the great outdoors the spider didn't need any encouragement, practically leaping to its freedom.

Kent pulled the stick inside and took two strides to the

window, pulling it shut. 'There. Happy now?' he asked as he turned around.

Sadie felt a sudden release of tension from her neck muscles as relief buzzed through her system. She might even have smiled had not her thong been dangling from the curtain rail just behind his head. It made her aware of their state of undress. Of his ripped naked chest. Of his perfect mouth surrounded by fascinating stubble.

Of how it would feel to kiss him.

She nodded instead, focusing only on him. 'Thank you,' she said, one hand at her throat, the other still clutching her clothes. 'I'll be able to sleep easy now.'

Kent grunted. With a vision of her in that towel and a pink thong, he certainly wouldn't be.

He walked out of the bathroom, brushing past her on the way out. 'Just get dressed, Sadie Bliss,' he muttered and headed back to his beer.

When Sadie emerged from the bathroom a couple of minutes later the television was on and Kent was reclining against the bed head, still in just his jeans, his feet bare. Both his legs were out in front of him, his right ankle crossed over the left. He held his beer tucked close to his body, resting against his groin area. He was channel surfing.

He turned the volume down a little but deliberately didn't look at her as he said, 'I can turn it off if it's going to keep you awake.'

She shook her head, ignoring the nice delineation of abdominal muscles and the fascinating trail of hair bisecting them. 'No, it's fine. I sleep like a log.'

Sadie lifted her backpack to the ground and pulled back the sheets. Uncaring that her hair was wet and tomorrow it would be a wild tangle, she slipped between them, enjoying their fresh clean feel and smell. Not even the rock-hard mattress spoilt the moment.

She half moaned, half sighed. 'God, that feels good.'

Kent, still looking resolutely at the television screen didn't bother to reply. It was bad enough her low moan completely destroyed his concentration.

'Night,' she said, pulling the sheets up to her chin, rolling away from him as she obeyed the dictates of her brain to shut her eyes and sleep.

Kent took a swig of his beer. He couldn't believe that anyone could just fall instantly asleep. He turned his head to look at her, the steady rise and fall of the sheet seeming to indicate that Sadie Bliss could.

How he envied her that. He hadn't had a decent night's sleep since the accident. Before that even. Living in war zones was not conducive to the recommended eight hours. And these days he barely got by on four or five.

A knock heralded the arrival of his food and he was grateful for something to do to fill up the long hours ahead.

Kent was relieved when Sadie finally moved five hours later. He was beginning to wonder if she'd lapsed into a coma. If it weren't for her regular deep breathing and the occasional soft, snuffly snore, he'd have checked her pulse hours ago.

He, on the other hand, was still well and truly awake. He'd eaten his steak, drunk two more beers, ordered them some breakfast on a card he'd hung on the outside door-knob, gone through his camera gear again, fiddled with the air-conditioning thermostat several times trying to find a happy medium and consulted the map at least half a dozen times.

He'd watched some B-grade movie and reruns of eight-ies sit-coms for hours. And now he was flicking between channels, avoiding the twenty-four-hour news stations in favour of twenty-four-hour infomercials.

Sadie flopping onto her back was a welcome distraction. Her head had rolled his way, the light flickering from the television throwing her face into interesting relief. Her skin looked even paler in the glow and long shadows fell on her cheeks from her eyelashes. Her delectable full mouth also eerily pale in the ghostly television glow seemed pursed as if ready for action.

His gaze drifted down. The sheet had ridden low exposing her T-shirt. Her perfectly plain, high-necked, nothing remotely provocative T-shirt. Hell, she was even wearing a bra! But that didn't obscure the fascinating bloom of her breasts, large and round and perfect, tenting the shirt, stretching it across their expanse. His eyes followed the line of the shirt as it fell again towards the flat of her ribs and the slight rise of her belly and he could just make out a thin strip of creamy skin before the sheet covered the rest of her.

His gaze drifted up again as he contemplated what she'd look like without the shirt. And the sheet. Would her nipples be pale too, like the rest of her, or would they be darker, closer to the colour of her mouth?

What would they taste like?

His groin stirred.

Then she moved, murmured something unintelligible, flung an arm above her head.

Kent looked away hurriedly.

What the hell was the matter with him? Perving on a woman whilst she slept? Imagining her naked. Like some oversexed teenager? Like some perverted stalker.

The number of things that were wrong with this scenario bought him to his feet. He rummaged through his bag, found some shorts and a T-shirt, dragged his shoes back on, grabbed the room key and headed out of the door.

Unlike Sydney, which never seemed to sleep, Cunnamulla at one in the morning was deserted. Nothing was open, no lights were on, no traffic rattled by as Kent launched himself into the cool night air with vigour. He pounded the pavements of the sleepy little town for an hour with only the occasional bark from a dog for company.

The physio had recommended he started light jogging as soon as the orthopod had cleared him five months ago and, like everything he did in life, Kent adopted it with gusto. It had helped to strengthen his right ankle significantly but it had also been a useful tool to cope with his insomnia. The accompanying exhaustion usually resulted in good quality sleep, unlike the other alternatives—alcohol and pills.

Beer and sleeping tablets certainly got him off to sleep very effectively but it was fitful and haunted by the things he could keep at bay during the day. The cries of Dwayne Johnson begging for his mother. The smell of jet fuel. The searing heat of nearby flames.

He seemed to wake more exhausted than he went to bed. And hung over to boot.

Running was far, far preferable.

Sadie was still sleeping soundly when he let himself back into the room. He barely looked at her as he headed for the bathroom. He shut the door, stripped off his clothes, turned the taps on and stepped into the spray. He closed his eyes, braced his outstretched arms against the wall, dropped his head, letting the water run over his neck for a while.

When he finally lifted his head and opened his eyes,

the pink thong hanging from the curtain rail was the first thing he saw.

He turned the cold on full blast.

Sadie woke to a knock at the door at seven o'clock. She opened her eyes. A tray with empty plates, used cutlery and three beer bottles greeted her and beyond that was Kent. He was curled up in his bed, sound asleep. His face was relaxed, his cheekbones not so pronounced, the creases around his mouth smoothed out, his lips slack and innocent rather than distinct and wicked.

He looked much, much younger.

He was still shirtless, the sheet pulled low on his abdomen and twisted around his legs. His right leg from the knee down was exposed and her gaze came to rest on his grossly deformed ankle.

The knock came again and he stirred.

Sadie jumped out of bed. 'Coming,' she called walking past the still flickering television on her way to the door. She opened it to the woman from last night bearing a smile and a tray.

'Good morning,' she chirped. 'Your breakfast.'

'Oh,' Sadie said, taking the laden tray. 'Er, thank you.'

Kent woke to the voices and rolled onto his back. His eyes felt gritty. It had taken another hour of infomercials before he'd finally fallen asleep after his shower, but he was used to having to wake and be instantly ready so he vaulted upright instead.

Sadie backed into the room, pushing the door shut with her foot, and turned around. She met Kent's bleary gaze. 'You ordered this, I assume?'

He nodded. 'Breakfast is the most important meal of the day.' He patted the bed. 'Put it here.'

Sadie plonked it where he indicated. She lifted the metallic covering on one of the plates. A full cooked breakfast greeted her—bacon, eggs, sausages, fried onions, tomatoes, and baked beans.

Her stomach growled at the waft of cooked meat and she started to salivate.

Her fat cells did too.

It looked so damn good. But she knew she couldn't indulge. In just a few shorts days her pants were already looser. And she'd be seeing Leo soon.

She replaced the lid and picked up one of the pieces of perfectly browned toast. 'Thanks,' she said, nibbling at the dry corner.

Kent scrunched his face as he looked up at her. She was wearing some baggy yoga-style pants to go with her baggy T-shirt. It was the unsexiest get-up he'd seen in his life. But even it didn't manage to keep the curvy figure beneath in check.

The curvy figure she was obviously trying to straighten out by depriving it of adequate nutrition. *That was it?* She was just going to eat one piece of dry toast?

'You don't want any more?'

'I never eat much breakfast,' Sadie lied as she bent over slightly and poured herself a cup of tea from the small metal teapot with a leaking lid. 'Usually just need a cuppa and I'm good.'

Her gaze flicked to his momentarily but she quickly looked away. She didn't expect or want him to know about the demons that drove her to this crash diet.

She doubted a he-man of his ilk would understand.

Their enforced proximity was bad enough without laying herself totally bare to him.

Kent watched as she pulled her gaze away and her hair swung back and forth across her shoulders at the activity.

It was a tangle of waves this morning. As if she'd spent the night in a wind tunnel.

'And I suppose you're going to eat nothing but celery and salads again today?'

Sadie sat cross-legged on her bed, facing the television. A news show was on. 'Carrots, actually,' she said primly.

Kent stared at her for a moment, then shook his head. He was on a road trip with a rabbit. He'd never understood women who obsessed over what they perceived to be every figure flaw and every calorie they shoved in their mouths. He'd dated his share and they were, without exception, boring.

And Sadie not realising just how gorgeous she looked was nothing short of criminal. Was she anorexic?

Or just screwed up by one too many magazine covers?

Kent eyed the piece of toast that she was nibbling, contemplating his next words carefully because he wanted to say them, to get involved in this juvenile silliness, about as much as he wanted to saw off the top of his head. But maybe she was like this because no one in her life had ever sat her down and told her that she had a smoking-hot body.

Although God alone knew what was wrong with men of her age today—were they blind or just incredibly stupid?

'Look, this is nothing to do with me and you can eat… or not eat…whatever you want but—and I say this with absolutely no disrespect or sexual harassment or icky older-man creepiness in mind—your body is fine.'

Sadie blinked. If that was a compliment it could sure do with some work. And gave her an opportunity to steer the conversation away from what she was and wasn't eating.

'Wow. You really are rusty,' she murmured.

Kent shot her an impatient look. 'I'm not here to stroke your ego, Sadie Bliss.' Or land himself in the middle of a lawsuit.

Or something else entirely inappropriate.

'Well, that's just as well because you'd be failing, Kent Nelson. You do know when you tell a woman her body is *fine* she interprets that as *you're okay but you could look better*, right? Unless, of course, you prefix it. *Mighty* fine or *damn* fine work quite well.'

The sad truth was Sadie knew that none of those prefixes applied. A few years back, when she'd been with Leo, mighty fine had fitted the bill. Now she was just struggling to keep back the tide.

Kent stared at her. Did she really think he gave a rat's arse about the female interpretation of fine? He shook his head. 'I don't suppose you have a clue how very much I *don't* care about the word fine? You do know that there's a whole heap of bad things happening out there in the world, right?' he growled.

'Really?' she snapped, tired of his paternalistic carry-on. 'I hadn't noticed, being a *journalist* and all.'

Kent glared, feeling exasperation rising in his throat threatening to choke him. *Why couldn't women just take a compliment in the spirit it was intended?*

'All I'm trying to say,' he said, swallowing hard against the lump, trying to get the conversation back on track, 'is you really need to eat better. You could get sick.'

Sadie wasn't prepared for such a left-field comment. For a man who obviously thought her figure concerns didn't rate compared to bigger global issues—which of course they didn't—his apparent concern for her was unexpected.

And he did look concerned. It softened the beautiful harshness of his mouth and her mind went blank for a moment as she tried to remember why she was so het up.

She sighed as her brain came back on line. 'Look, I'm fine. I promise. It's just…complicated, okay? And it's really none of your business. So can we please drop it?'

She did not want to get into this with a man as accomplished as Kent. How could he possibly understand what was personally at stake for her over seeing Leo again? How much she had to prove.

Kent held her gaze, the appeal luminous in her large grey eyes. Her *back the hell off* polite considering their recent exchange.

Complicated he understood.

And she was right, it wasn't his business. And what did he care if some crazy chick in well-to-do Australia chose to forgo food that millions of women would lay down their lives for just so they could feed their children for a few more days?

'Sure,' he agreed, pulling the metal covering off his cooked breakfast as he inhaled the rich aroma of meat and onions. Sadie Bliss was a transient connection in his life. If she chose to starve, then so be it. He sure as hell wasn't.

He'd been in too many places where food was scarce to not appreciate the bounty in front of him.

He picked up his fork and tucked in.

Sadie resolutely tried to ignore Kent annihilating his coronary-bypass plate with gusto. But it smelled so damn good it was hard to concentrate on anything else. Add to that his naked chest and it was a regular double feature. She tried to follow the news programme but what was going on in her peripheral vision was much more interesting.

After a while, though, she became aware of something else. Kent, eating with one hand, gently massaging his injured ankle with the other. He seemed engrossed alternately in his meal and the television so she didn't think he was even aware he was doing it.

She slid surreptitious looks his way. The ankle looked pretty smashed up and the top of his foot had a chunk missing, a smooth shiny piece of bright pink skin lay over top as if it had been grafted. He looked her way and caught her watching.

She held his gaze. 'Does it hurt?' she asked.

Kent frowned for a moment, wondering what she was talking about, then realised he was rubbing his ankle. He'd overdone it slightly with the run and it was suffering a little this morning.

Normally he would have told her to mind *her* business but her simple enquiry caught him off guard. Too often people asked him what had happened, pried and pushed for all the gory details.

But not Sadie Bliss.

She'd simply asked him if it hurt.

He looked down at the foot he'd come so close to losing on several occasions, his fingers massaging the ridged scar tissue, the dips and planes of the deformed joint. 'It aches sometimes.' He shrugged. 'It's just habit really.'

Sadie nodded. Weren't they all just creatures of habit?

CHAPTER FOUR

'So, WHERE to today?' Sadie asked as she vaulted up into the passenger seat an hour later.

The roads, now they were hitting the outback proper, tended to be long stretches of straight with very few curves or bends so she figured she was safe to take the passenger seat again.

'Mt Isa,' Kent said as he pulled out of the hotel car park. 'It's about thirteen hours. That'll leave only a nine-ish-hour drive tomorrow to Borroloola.'

Sadie nodded. 'I'll give Leo a ring from the hotel tonight and let him know to expect us.'

Kent quirked an eyebrow. 'Leo?'

Sadie mentally chastised herself for the slip. But she smiled at Kent calmly and said, 'Mr Pinto.'

Kent wasn't buying it. 'Leo's very…familiar,' he pushed. 'I hear he's only Leo to his friends.'

Sadie looked out of the window as they left the last of Cunnamulla behind. 'Is he?'

Kent considered her deliberate evasion, intrigued despite himself. Which was just as well. Seeing that thong last night had tripped some kind of switch in his head. And he didn't like where it was taking him. Maybe the Pinto/Bliss conundrum would give him something else to think about other than Sadie oozing curves and sex all over the passenger seat.

'Thirteen hours is a long time to stay silent, Sadie Bliss. I bet you can't even manage two.'

Sadie looked back at him, ignoring his deliberate baiting. 'Why do you say my name like that?' she diverted.

'What? Sadie Bliss?'

She listened as he said it again, rolling it around his tongue like a particularly delicious morsel. She imagined what that tongue could do to certain parts of her anatomy and muscles deep in her belly went into free fall.

He shrugged. 'Sensational byline. Very rockstar. Is it real?'

Sadie rolled her eyes at the familiarity of the question. 'Yes. Just like my boobs and my lips it's one hundred per cent real.'

Kent flicked a glance at her. She was glaring at him with exasperation. 'Okay, okay,' he said because, no matter what, there wasn't one iota of that conversation he was going anywhere near.

Sadie deliberately ticked down the minutes until two hours were up before turning to Kent and yanking on his ear bud.

'Let's make a deal,' she said.

Kent raised an eyebrow. 'Bet that was the longest two hours of your life.'

'Nope. Two minutes in a bathroom with a mutant spider was much longer.'

'Okay, so let's see if we can go another two, shall we?' he suggested as he located his swinging ear bud.

Sadie shook her head. 'We're not going to sit here all day and not talk to each other again.'

Kent flicked a glance at her, then back at the road. 'We're not?'

Sadie shook her head. 'It's ridiculous.'

Kent shrugged. 'It was working for me.'

She folded her arms. 'Have I mentioned how very annoying I can be when I set my mind to it?'

Kent didn't doubt it. He remembered how she'd harped on about the spider last night until he'd hunted the poor thing from the room. 'You mean you haven't set it already?'

She ignored him. 'We'll just agree on a subject and stick to the boundaries of it.'

He eyed her warily. 'Like what?'

She shrugged. 'How about starting at the beginning? Our childhoods?'

Kent considered it for a moment. It was a safe topic. No skeletons to hide. It could be a good trade for some peace and quiet. He reached for a packet of potato chips he had left over from yesterday. 'Okay,' he agreed, opening them as he drove along. 'But then I get silence for the rest of the day.'

Sadie shook her head, ignoring the aroma of carbohydrates, leaning forward to grab the carrot sticks she'd chopped earlier. 'For another two hours,' she bargained.

Kent tapped his fingers on the wheel. 'Mid-afternoon.'

'Lunchtime,' she returned without even taking a breath.

'After lunch,' he clarified.

Sadie considered it for a moment. It was better than nothing. She nodded at him and then launched straight into it. 'So, what's the Kent Nelson story?'

Kent kept his eyes trained on the road as he munched on chips. 'Not a lot to tell.'

She laughed at that and Kent blinked as he realised he hadn't heard it before. Her laughter was deep and throaty and he found himself utterly intrigued. It wasn't tittery or tinkly or musical like so many of the women he knew.

It was full roar, like the rest of her. So few people, especially the places he'd been, laughed with every fibre of their being.

But Sadie Bliss did.

It was strangely soothing in the cocoon of the cab.

'Right,' she said. 'Of course not. World renowned, multi-award-winning photojournalist who's been in every war zone on the planet in the last decade. But nothing here to see, folks, move along?'

'Okay, how about not a lot I want to talk about?'

Sadie regarded him for a moment. His jaw was clenched just beneath his cheekbone, his brow was scrunched. 'We made a deal,' she reminded him.

'Oh, well, in that case…'

She didn't miss the sarcasm in his arid tone but she wasn't going to be put off by it either. 'Tell me about your parents. I'd appreciate a tale of divorce and woe if you have one?'

Kent glanced at her to gauge her sincerity. She seemed fairly matter-of-fact. ''Fraid not. Two parents, both still together and very much in love. An older sister. Standard Australian suburban upbringing.'

Sadie liked the sound of that. 'They must be proud of you,' she murmured.

He shrugged. 'Worried mostly.'

The minute he'd taken off for the Middle East over a decade ago his family had worried. He didn't know how many times his mother had called the foreign affairs department if he missed a scheduled call in, but he was pretty sure she had a direct line at one stage.

And then, since the accident, they'd been even more concerned.

'I suppose you were an angelic child,' Sadie mused.

'Straight As. House captain. School newspaper. Valedictorian.'

Kent burst out laughing. He couldn't help it. She was so far wide of the target she was practically off the page. 'No. I think my mother once described me to one of my many school principals, in my presence, as a horrible little shit.'

Sadie blinked. At the admission and his laughter. It was just as delicious as last night. Low and easy, it transformed the spare planes of his face into a pallet of lines and creases. It softened his mouth and twinkled in his eyes. 'And were you?'

He glanced at her. 'Guilty as charged.'

Sadie wasn't quite sure what to say. He certainly didn't look contrite. He'd just described an idyllic childhood— one she would have killed for. What on earth had motivated him to behave in such a way that his own mother would disparage him?

'Because they didn't understand you and you were trying to prove something or some other lame excuse that horrible little boys make to justify their behaviour?' she asked sweetly.

Kent laughed again but it was more brittle. 'No. I guess I just always craved adventure. Wanted to know what was beyond the end of my street. Outside my town. Over the sea. On the other side of the world. I'm afraid I became a bit of a hell raiser as I chafed against the bonds of my perfectly nice, domesticated, suburban life.'

Somehow Sadie could imagine that. Especially with the whole buzz cut and bristles he had going on. It seemed more in line with the whole *he-man* thing than the safe middle-class life he'd just described.

'So you what? Broke some rules, got caught shoplifting, maybe smoking behind the bike sheds? Some trouble with the cops?' She snuck a look at him. 'Caught a venereal disease?'

Kent almost choked at her suggestions. 'Hell, no,' he spluttered.

'No to the venereal disease?' she asked innocently.

He pierced her with a quelling look. 'No to any of them.'

'Well, what then?' she demanded.

Kent looked back to the road as Sadie's mouth pouted the question at him. 'I wagged school. Constantly. Spent my time at the arcade or swimming at the local creek. I did crazy things like jumping off buildings and sticking my hand into an ants' nest and climbing to the top of an electricity pylon.'

Sadie blinked. 'Why would you do those things?'

Kent looked at her. 'Because someone dared me to.'

'Oh.'

She'd never really understood boys. She hadn't had a brother—or not one that she'd known as she was growing up anyway. And her father had always seemed a bit of a mystery to her. The same went for the men she'd dated. Even the ones she'd slept with. She'd understood them as sexual beings but the rest was a mystery.

Even Leo, probably the least he-man guy she'd ever known, had this stubborn male pride about him.

Ego, she supposed some psychologists would call it.

'They sound kind of dangerous.'

Kent nodded, his eyes fixed on the road. 'I always had something in plaster. My poor mother became an expert at taking out stitches. A couple of times she even threatened to put them in herself, with no local anaesthetic.'

'Maybe she should have?' Sadie suggested.

He chuckled. 'I do believe my father proposed it on several occasions.'

'So…rattling around in war zones? That took care of

the adventure cravings?' she asked. She was pushing it but it was a natural segue and he finally seemed conducive to being pushed.

'Yes.' Kent sobered a little as he realised he'd answered a question that had strayed off topic.

'Are you going back?' she asked.

There was a beat where he looked as if he was going to answer her and Sadie held her breath. Then he reached into his chip packet, pulled one out and tossed it into his mouth.

He glanced at her. 'How do you know Leo?'

Sadie gave him a grudging smile. He'd retreated back behind his line. And she had absolutely no intention of coming out from behind hers.

They were back to the beginning again.

An hour later Kent pulled the vehicle into a petrol station to stock up on more calorie-laden essentials. They'd passed that time in silence again, his MP3 player firmly plugged into his ear canals.

He hadn't asked her any questions about her childhood and Sadie felt a little miffed.

Surely he was a little interested in *her* childhood?

'I bought extra,' Kent announced as he dumped a plastic bag between them.

She was wearing pretty much the same type of outfit as yesterday—cut-offs and a loose polo shirt. He wasn't quite sure what she was trying to achieve in denying her curves the artistic outlet they deserved but he'd hate to see them starved into oblivion.

Sadie shot him a sweet smile through gritted teeth as the vehicle got back onto the highway. 'Imagine my surprise,' she said as she bit into a carrot stick with a loud crunch.

Of course the crunch of breaking wafer biscuit as he bit

into a chocolate bar was far more satisfying. Especially followed by a waft of something sweet.

Chocolate?

Sugar...

A smear of caramel clung to that beautiful full lower lip and Sadie turned away from the decadent scene. Kent Nelson eating a chocolate bar should come with an obscenity warning!

She munched on a handful of carrots sticks and ignored him for a while. They staved off the grumbles but were hardly satisfying. Kent licking his lips in her peripheral vision did not help.

'So, you want to hear my story now?' she asked.

Kent didn't look at her as he shook his head. 'Not really.'

Sadie blinked at his rejection. The implication that she wasn't remotely interesting stung. And besides, she needed to keep him talking, not least of all because the silence was driving her crazy. 'But you told me yours.'

He shrugged. 'I like hearing mine.'

Narcissist. 'It's only polite to listen to the other person's story, you know? It's called conversation.'

Kent eyeballed her. 'I don't suppose there's any way you're letting this drop, is there?'

Sadie gave her head a firm shake. 'Nope.'

He took a deep breath. *Fine.* 'So tell me, how was it growing up? Blissful?'

Sadie ignored the wisecrack. It wasn't as if she hadn't heard it before. She looked out of her window at the dry yellow-green scenery flashing by. 'Not so much, as it turned out. My dad up and left when I was twelve and got himself a new family. With his secretary. Spreading the bliss...as you do.'

Kent whistled. 'Ouch.'

Sadie nodded. Ouch all right. She still remembered the

day he'd left. Coming home from school to her mother crying. Trying to comprehend what had happened. That her father had been so unhappy he'd left her. Just walked away. The years of trying to hold onto him, trying to make him love her all for nothing.

'Do you have a relationship with him?'

'Of sorts,' she murmured. 'I have two half-brothers. Twins. I see them, ergo I see him.'

Kent thought about how close he was with his own father. 'That seems kind of…distant.'

'Well…I never really quite measured up. He was a bit of a jock who'd wanted a boy. Someone he could take to the footy and the cricket. And—' she lifted a shoulder '—he got me. Who liked to read. And draw. And daydream. I'm afraid I was a bit of a disappointment. I spent a lot of years trying to be who he wanted me to be but I never quite got there and then the twins came along and…'

Kent nodded. 'He had someone to take to the footy.'

Bingo. 'Yes.'

Not even the engine of the Land Rover, loud by modern standards, could drown out the wistful note in Sadie's voice. 'And your mother?'

'Mum's great. She's been a rock. Through everything. She could have become bitter, but she wasn't. She just got a part-time job and supported me in everything I wanted to do. When I went to art college she took on a second job to pay my tuition.'

Kent looked at her. 'Art college?'

Sadie nodded as she transferred her attention back to the blur of the outback. 'I wanted to be an artist for a while.'

She shook her head even as she said it. What had she been thinking?

Kent flicked his gaze to the road, then back to her. 'What medium?'

Sadie ironed the flat of her palms down the fabric of her fake cammo cut-offs. 'Painting.'

'What happened?'

She twined a finger into her hair. *I met Leo.* 'I wasn't really that talented.' She shrugged. 'I dropped out.'

Became someone else's muse instead.

Kent frowned at her nonchalance. There was a hell of a lot more to that story!

None of which he wanted to know.

'So you became a journo? A bit different from painting, surely?'

'Not really. I paint my pictures with words now. I like it. I like the facts of it, the clearly defined boundaries. Art is all about interpretation. You must know that,' she said dismissively, looking up at him. 'Reporting deals in definites, in absolutes. I like the structure.'

She did. She really did.

Art for her had been a double-edged sword. So tied in with her emotions, her well-being, it had been hard to separate out. It had felt like possession.

Which was, as Leo had pointed out, insane when her talent didn't justify it.

It had certainly destroyed her relationship with him.

'Don't you miss the creativity?'

Sadie shook her head. 'Words are creative,' she countered.

Kent shot her a *come-on-now* look. 'You know what I mean.' He'd thought for a long time he never wanted to get behind a camera again, but the urge had returned with gusto.

Sadie sighed, fixing her gaze on distant hills. 'Painting took over my life. Or rather striving to be good enough took over my life.' Leo had been a hard taskmaster when she'd gone to live with him and trying to get it right had been impossible. 'I'm afraid if I took it up again I'd be back in that place. I don't think I can have one without the other.'

'Well, that sounds intense,' he murmured.

'Trust me—' she grimaced '—it was.'

Kent's fingers tightened around the wheel. 'Did you paint nudes?' he asked, wondering suddenly if that was where the Pinto puzzle pieces fitted.

Sadie pulled her gaze off the horizon, not that far gone that she didn't recognise he'd moved her into dangerous territory.

'Where should we stop for lunch, do you think?' she asked, pulling the map out of the glovebox.

They stopped for lunch at a truck stop near Blackall. Sadie ate a ham and salad roll but discarded the bun. Kent watched as she leaned forward slightly when his hamburger with beetroot and a fried egg arrived as if she was trying to absorb its mouth-watering aroma. He was also aware of her gaze as he brought it to his mouth and chomped into the juicy delight.

When the waitress delivered his lamington and large caramel thick shake to the table he thought he almost heard her whimper before she stood abruptly.

'I'll wait for you by the car,' she said.

Kent watched her go. Her wavy hair swung between her shoulder blades, her shirt hung loose around her waist and bottom, completely concealing everything down to the backs of her thighs. But every time she moved those curves moved with her and there wasn't one trucker in the joint that didn't watch her sway out of the door.

He continued to watch her through the glass sliding doors as she walked out into the heat of the midday sun and strolled towards the vehicle. She looked up at a massive road train semi-trailer thundering past. The guy driving was hanging out his window, leering and yelling something at Sadie.

Kent wasn't an expert lip-reader but he did pretty well with body language so he figured that when Sadie flipped the bird, the trucker had probably suggested she flash him a certain part of her anatomy.

He sucked the last of the thick icy shake up his straw and watched his fellow diners, who were looking wistfully at Sadie no doubt wishing that she'd complied with the lewd request.

The woman was a walking, talking hourglass. Why was she so hell-bent on straitjacketing her assets? Why did she want to starve them into submission?

Kent stood, throwing a tip on the table.

It was none of his bloody business.

Halfway between Barcaldine and Longreach they blew a tyre. Sadie was in a deep sleep when Kent's curse woke her.

'What's up?' she asked as he pulled off onto the side of the highway.

'Got a flat.' He turned off the engine. 'Sit tight. I'll have it fixed in a jiffy.'

Sadie blinked as lingering sleepiness tugged at her eyelids. Broken sleep made her irritable and his *he-man* condescension grated. 'What makes you think I can't have it done in a jiffy?' she grouched as he opened his door. 'I am perfectly capable of changing a tyre, you know?'

Kent raised his hands in surrender. 'You want to do it? Knock yourself out. I'm all for women's lib.'

If she wanted to get hot and dirty he wasn't going to stop her. Of course, she wouldn't be able to undo the wheel nuts but it might be fun watching her try.

Sadie jumped down to the ground and looked around.

The scenery hadn't changed much for hours. Flat, dry, brittle pastures with the slightest tinge of green. And lots of sheep. It was quiet out here apart from the occasional rattle of a passing car.

'Where are we?' she asked when she joined him to look at the shredded back passenger tyre.

''Bout half an hour out of Longreach,' he said, kicking the flat in disgust. He'd put four new tyres on the vehicle before coming away. 'We'll get the tyre repaired there.'

He walked to the back and opened the doors. Sadie helped him move their gear onto the ground so he could access the spare tyre.

'How long will that take?' Making this trip any longer wasn't particularly thrilling.

'Hopefully they'll be able to do it for us straight away. Maybe a delay of an hour?' He located the wheel brace and handed it to her. 'Why don't you get started while I grab the spare?'

Sadie saw the challenge in his eyes and gave him a triumphant smile. A man who'd always wanted a son had been a useful person to have around when she was learning to drive—Sadie had changed many a tyre, thanks to her father.

She approached the job with a spring in her step. It would be good to teach *he-man* that she was a little more than a neurotic, food-obsessed girly.

And it was a perfect plan until she hit the first hurdle. None of the wheel nuts would budge. When Kent brought the spare around she was cursing and muttering under her breath, practically standing on the brace trying to shift one of the stubborn nuts.

'Would you like a hand?' he asked innocently.

She glared at him. 'Why on earth are these on so tight? You'd need to be Popeye on steroids to get them undone.'

He grinned. 'They tighten the nuts with a machine.'

'Well, that seems kind of stupid, doesn't it, if people can't get them off?'

He nodded, trying to be serious. 'Of course, maybe if you'd eaten a burger for lunch you might be feeling stronger.'

'I would have to have eaten an entire side of beef to be strong enough to take these suckers off.' She thrust the brace at him in disgust. 'Looks like it's a job for *he-man*.'

Kent suppressed the urge to cough at her forceful handing over of the tool. 'Step aside.'

Sadie watched, her pride soothed as Kent had to use significant grunt to shift the nuts. Still, he made pretty short work of the tyre change and was cleaning off greasy hands in less than fifteen minutes.

He had sweat and grease on his forehead and the testosterone cloud emanating from him was making her dizzy. She opened the back passenger door and handed him a bottle of cold water from the supply in the camp-fridge.

'Thanks,' Kent said, twisting the lid and guzzling half in one swallow before pouring some over his head.

Sadie's gaze followed rivulets of water as they trekked over the contours of his face, his mouth and down the tanned column of his neck.

She reached in and grabbed one for herself.

A breeze lifted her hair as she slaked her thirst and put out a few fires south of her throat. Lusting after Kent was just plain counterproductive. She had a job to do here and it didn't have anything to do with her sexy photographer.

She didn't need another complication.

Leo was complicated enough.

She lounged back against the vehicle, ignoring Kent, who was doing the same. She looked out over the outback vista instead. It seemed flat all the way to the horizon, interrupted only by the odd clump of trees and the occasional fence. The only population appeared to be sheep and the odd passing car.

There was something soothing about the isolation.

In the distance she saw the beginning of something that looked like a brown dust cloud barrelling along close to the ground and parallel with the road. 'What's that?' she asked.

Kent squinted to where she was pointing. It was too far away to see properly but, given that it was travelling at a rate of knots, it wouldn't be long before it was passing by. 'Not sure,' he said, reaching into the back passenger foot well and removing his camera bag.

He pulled out his camera, clicked on the zoom lens and looked through it. He smiled as the cloud took form and shape.

'Emus,' he announced.

Sadie stared as the cloud came closer and she could just make out individual figures. 'So it is,' she murmured. 'Wow, look at them go!'

A flock of about a dozen of the large, flightless birds was running helter-skelter, their powerful legs eating up the paddock, their feet kicking up dirt and dust, their soft feathers bouncing with each foot fall. As they got closer still Sadie counted ten of them.

Even with them way out in the paddock when they passed by, they were a magnificent sight. 'Where are they going?' she mused out loud.

'Who knows?' Kent shrugged as he snapped off a series of pictures. 'But they're in a hurry.'

They'd no sooner drawn nearer then they were past. 'That was amazing,' Sadie said, watching the cloud get smaller and smaller. 'I've never seen emus in the wild.'

He tisked. 'City chick,' he muttered as he continued to click away.

Sadie watched him as he peered through the lens—focused, centred. It reminded her of the picture she'd seen of him in New York, where the camera had seemed an extension of him. He stood, his whole body engaged in the process, as if he'd been born with a camera.

'When did you know you wanted to take pictures for a living?'

Kent ignored her, snapping until the birds were no longer distinguishable. When he pulled the camera away from his face he looked down at Sadie. His first instinct was to shut her down, as he had been doing, but the camera felt good in his hand, the pictures he'd just taken felt right and he remembered the first time so vividly.

'I was sixteen. My grandfather took me on a road trip to the Red Centre during the school holidays. His camera was ancient but it took amazing images.'

Sadie thought how nice it would have been to have had a grandparent in her life. 'That was nice of him,' she mused.

Kent snorted. 'I think my mother was at the end of her tether and Grandad feared there would be bloodshed. I think he was just trying to save his daughter's sanity.'

He smiled, remembering that momentous trip. How it had changed his life.

He put the camera to his face again and scanned the broad canvas before him. 'There was something about the light out there,' he said. 'The contrasting colours. I was hooked.'

Sadie watched him peering through his lens. 'I bet your mother was relieved,' she murmured.

Kent gave a short sharp laugh as he lowered the camera. 'Hell, yeah. She signed me up for a photography course as soon as I got back.'

Sadie sucked in a breath at the smile that transformed the harsh planes of his face. He really ought to do it more often. 'And you never gave her a spot of bother again?' she predicted.

He nodded. He had knuckled down. Once he'd found his calling he'd put his all into achieving his goal. 'Essentially,' he agreed as he returned his camera to its bag in the back of the car. 'The war zone thing kind of freaked her out.'

Sadie nodded. 'Mums worry. That's their job, I guess.'

Her mother had worried about her too. About how she'd tried so hard to be the boy her father wanted. Tried even harder to be the woman Leo wanted. She'd been especially concerned at Sadie's obsession with her figure.

Kent looked down at the pensive look on her face. She seemed to have gone somewhere far away, a little frown knitting her brows together, her teeth torturing that perfect bottom lip.

'Come on,' he said, stepping back from her. And her mouth. 'We better get this show on the road if we want to get to Mt Isa before this day is over.'

They got to Mt Isa at eleven that night after a couple of stops for photos. They'd passed the hours with minimal conversation despite Sadie's best efforts.

'How are you feeling?' Kent asked as he pulled into a petrol station. 'Tired?'

Sadie shook her head. Strangely she wasn't. Driving through the eerily flat landscape on a cloudless, practically moonless night had been weirdly energising. As if she were in a spaceship, floating through the cosmos.

'You want to see if we can make the Northern Territory border? It's another couple of hours but it'll cut the trip down tomorrow. We can pull off to the side of the road and catch a few hours' kip before moving on.'

Sadie regarded him for a minute. 'Pull over? And where do we sleep?'

'I'll take my swag up to the roof of the vehicle and sleep under the stars. You can doss down on the back seat if you like.'

She pursed her lips. 'Camping, huh?'

Kent shot her a derisive look. 'I'd hardly call it that. But it's something you should try at least once in your life.'

Sadie looked at him. At his mouth.

Her, him and a billion stars.

And his mouth.

'Okay.'

CHAPTER FIVE

'ARE you coming up or not?'

Sadie stood with her hands on the bull bar as an outback night stretched dark and mysterious like a lucky eight ball above her head.

It was one a.m. and they were pulled over near the dust-encrusted sign that announced their entry into the Northern Territory. It was chilly and she shivered.

'Are you sure it's okay to walk on your car? Won't it get dinged?'

Kent shut his eyes, blocking out the pinpricks of light twinkling down at him. 'If it was one of those modern four-wheel drives, sure. But this thing wasn't built to crumple. It was built to deflect.'

Sadie eyed the bonnet dubiously even though she knew how sturdy it was from the way it handled. Walking on a car just didn't seem right.

'By my reckoning I have you by a good twenty-five to thirty kilos, Sadie Bliss, and it didn't buckle under my weight. Unless of course you want to stay on the ground there and fend off the spiders.'

Sadie's pulse spiked as she leapt onto the bull bar. Her gaze flicked from side to side. 'There are spiders?'

Kent opened his eyes and grinned at the strained note in her voice. 'Probably a few scorpions too, I'd say.'

Sadie shuddered. 'Now, see, this is why I don't camp. There aren't any scorpions at five-star hotels,' she griped.

'There aren't any up here either,' he said, too tired for hysterics.

Sadie flicked her gaze from the ground to the roof of the car where she could just make out the outline of Kent's body encased in his swag. 'Think I'll just use the back seat,' she said, even though the thought of having to put her foot to the ground was creeping her out.

'Up to you. But, just so you know, you're missing out on a truly spectacular experience.' The celestial display was utterly dazzling and Kent wished he'd brought his camera up with him. 'It'll blow your mind, city girl.'

Sadie rolled her eyes and muttered, 'Yeah, yeah, that's what they all say,' under her breath. Except sound travelled exceptionally well through a still outback night and she blushed when she heard Kent chuckle.

'Okay,' she announced in a louder voice as she hauled herself onto the bonnet. 'But I'm going to want my money back if you're getting me up there under false pretences.'

Kent saluted. 'Money-back guarantee.'

Sadie kicked off her ballet flats and felt the warmth of the engine heat her cool toes as she clamoured gingerly to her feet. She gave a slight bounce, testing the strength of the metal beneath, satisfied to feel absolutely no give whatsoever.

She scrambled up the windscreen, hanging onto the sturdy metal rungs welded to the roof completely enclosing it. *At least she wouldn't roll off the roof in her sleep!* She rather inelegantly hauled herself up over the top and crawled on her hands and knees towards Kent and her swag.

She didn't look at him as she climbed into her bedding and zipped it up to her chin. She squeezed her eyes shut tight, hoping that she could block him and their sleeping arrangement out altogether. She was immediately cocooned in fleecy warmth, tiredness injecting instant fatigue into her marrow. She moved around for a bit attempting to find a comfortable spot, thankful for the swag's padded lining on the unforgiving metal rooftop.

'Will you stop wriggling,' Kent grumbled. He was actually feeling tired and there was something soothing about being outdoors. He planned on taking full advantage.

Sadie stopped moving and opened her eyes as the illusion that she wasn't on a car rooftop in the middle of the night, in the middle of nowhere, with a virtual stranger was completely obliterated by his gruff command.

And then a billion stars and a crescent moon took over and everything else melted away.

They had stars in Sydney. She'd often been out on the harbour at night and had them twinkle down at her, but somehow they just hadn't been able to compete with the ones twinkling from the buildings that made up Sydney's iconic skyline.

Not so tonight.

Tonight a New Year's Eve fireworks display would have paled in comparison.

The inky blackness blazed and dazzled as the lights from billions of stars glowed seemingly just for her. They crowded each other out, a black and white kaleidoscope, and on the roof of the car in the vast nothingness of the outback night, where the line between heaven and earth didn't exist, Sadie felt as if she could just reach up and pluck one from the cosmos.

Looking up, she suddenly understood how Van Gogh must have felt when he'd painted his famous starry French sky.

She breathed out. 'Wow.'

'Indeed,' Kent agreed, staring into the inky dome with her. 'You want your money back now?'

Sadie shook her head slowly. 'They're like…diamonds or crystals or teardrops or…something… I don't have the words.'

Kent grimaced. Unfortunately he did. They were the diamanté on Sadie's pink thong.

All trillion of them.

Winking down at him.

'Wow,' he murmured, trying to divert his thoughts from her underwear. 'Sadie Bliss lost for words. Somebody call a doctor.'

Sadie smiled as her gaze roamed the sky. 'Shut up, Kent Nelson. You're ruining the moment.'

Kent chuckled. 'I'll make a camper out of you yet.'

Sadie ignored him as a sudden revelation dawned. She might not be able to find the words but she knew exactly how she could express the swell of emotion swirling inside her. The urge to paint, to replicate what she saw on canvas, flowed through her on a surge of energy that fizzed and bubbled in her veins like a slug of Moët.

She hadn't felt it in a long time. Not since Leo had told her she'd only been awarded the scholarship to the London Art College because the director owed him a favour.

'Don't you want to take a picture of it?' she said quietly, not wanting to disturb the preternatural hush of the sleeping outback.

Kent glanced at her, surprised by the awe, the emotion in her voice. Her lips were slightly parted, the waning light from the crescent moon laid gentle fingers across the plush pillows.

He nodded as he fixed his gaze firmly heavenward again. 'Yes,' he admitted. 'I'll make sure I get some before the trip ends.'

Sadie wasn't sure how long they lay there just looking at the sky. She'd have never thought a person could actually stargaze and lose track of time. But her fingers were tingling and her mind was buzzing. How could she capture all this? Do it justice?

How could he?

But then she remembered his photograph in the exhibition—its very starkness the key to its power—and knew if anyone could, he could.

She was conscious of him awake beside her. She could hear his breath. Knew somehow that he, too, was looking at the cosmic vista with the eye of a true artist.

'I saw *Mortality*,' she said into the night. 'In New York. A few months back.'

Kent's gaze that had been roaming freely screeched to a halt directly above him. He didn't say anything. He didn't move a muscle. He barely breathed. He hadn't wanted that photo, any of the crash photos, to go public but the families of the men who'd died had specifically requested that they be released. And he hadn't been about to deny them.

Still, he'd had no idea that out of that day forged in hell his photograph of a dying soldier would leave a lasting mark on the world.

It was what every photojournalist dreamed of, he supposed, but it was an honour he could do without.

Sadie turned her head to look at his silent profile. He had one arm flung above him, propping his head a little higher. His mouth was a bleak slash adding to the severity of the rest of his face. His gaze was trained steadfastly above.

'It was…amazing. Did you see how well the gallery had it lit?'

Kent shook his head. 'I never go to my exhibitions.'

Sadie blinked, surprised. As an art student she'd survived on dreams of attending her own exhibitions. 'Well, they did a great job. Although it doesn't need much, does it? It's so…stark. Such a…private image. I had to leave. I couldn't look at it.'

Kent didn't want to talk about the photo. Especially not with a woman whose definition of a hard day was the presence of a rather large spider.

'Goodnight, Sadie Bliss,' he said, rolling away from her.

Then Sadie was staring at his back wishing she'd never said anything at all.

Sadie was momentarily confused when she startled awake some time later, her heart racing. She wasn't sure of the time but the stars were still out in force. She wasn't even sure what had woken her. Then Kent whimpered beside her and she knew.

She raised herself up on her elbow, her pulse still beating madly as he shook his head from side to side in his sleep, baring his gritted teeth. His swag had ridden down exposing his T-shirt-clad chest. His breath sawed in and out, harsh and loud in the stillness of the night.

'Kent?' she murmured.

He didn't respond, still obviously caught somewhere deep and dark inside his head. The same place the shadows came from, no doubt.

'Kent?' she said, louder this time.

Still nothing.

Another distressed little cry came from somewhere at the back of his throat, his face twisting as if he were in physical as well as mental agony, and before she could form a rational thought she was reaching out for him, placing her hand on his chest.

'Shh,' she murmured, rubbing the flat of her palm

against his chest, soothing him as she would one of her younger brothers. 'Shh.'

To her surprise, he quietened a little and she continued to gently pat his chest until the creases in his face flattened out, his beautiful mouth relaxed, his breathing settled.

She looked down at him as she absently patted him. What was going on inside his head? Was he reliving the helicopter crash that killed nine of the soldiers he'd been embedded with for almost two months? Was he hearing their cries? Did he see Dwayne Johnson's rosary beads and his grimy tear-streaked face every time he shut his eyes?

She had. For days after leaving the gallery it had played on her mind. And she'd only seen the photograph.

She hadn't been there when it had all gone down.

Had he talked to someone about it? Or didn't *he-men* believe in all that touchy-feely stuff?

Maybe he needed to, though. If he was suffering from PTSD it would be vital, surely? Even *he-men* needed help through such huge life upheavals.

The cool air swirling around her shoulders made her shiver and Sadie collapsed on her side, hunching down a little into her swag, keeping her palm anchored against his chest. She was reluctant to remove it despite Kent's now peaceful slumber. The steady thump of his heartbeat was firm and solid beneath her fingers, his chest expanded evenly and it was curiously reassuring.

Her gaze drifted to his face, relaxed now. She followed the hollows beneath his cheekbones to the beautiful symmetry of his mouth. Even slack with slumber it was utterly fascinating and for the first time in a long time she wished she had her sketch book with her. Once upon a time she'd never have gone anywhere without it.

And tonight with the stars and Kent's mouth she missed it desperately.

Movement in the distance caught her eye and she flicked her gaze just above his face to see the tail end of a shooting star heading towards the inky, barely discernible horizon.

She shut her eyes deciding what to wish upon. It should be something to do with Leo. A wish that he could see she had been a success without him. A wish that maybe he'd still want her. Just a little. That maybe he was still a little in love with her.

That he'd been pining for her.

But strangely on this night that Kent had given her she didn't want it to be about a man who had used her up and thrown her away.

So she wished Kent a dreamless sleep before drifting off herself.

Kent woke slowly to early daylight. The sun was still low and there was a heavy feeling against his chest. He gradually cracked his eyelids open, giving his pupils a chance to adjust.

It was quiet. So quiet. No muffled city traffic waking him. Not even insects to break the eerie morning stillness.

The sky, not yet fully warmed by the sun, was still a soft blue. He turned his head, inspecting the distant horizon. The line where the dome of the heavens met the arc of the earth was still a little hazy in the cool morning air. In an hour, when heat transformed blue sky and red dirt into almost unbearable vibrancy, the line would slash a distinct path between the two.

He looked down at his chest, surprised to find the heaviness there was a hand. Sadie's hand. He turned his head to look at her, his gaze meeting a river of hair, her back to him. He looked down at her hand again. No rings. No fingernail polish. None of those French manicures that every second woman seemed to sport these days. Just neatly trimmed nails, not too short, not too long.

Nothing fancy. Just like the rest of her.

Quite why she had her hand on his chest he wasn't sure. He knew from her loglike sleep in Cunnamulla she wasn't a restless sleeper. So why was she touching him?

And, more importantly, why was he just lying here not doing anything about it?

In the distance he could just make out the noise of a car approaching and as it got closer she started to stir. He froze as Sadie turned, rolled to face him, sighed, licked her gorgeous lips and then settled to sleep again.

All without moving her hand.

He held his breath as the car passed by without waking her and then he was looking right in her face, her plump mouth moist from the swipe of her tongue. The deep red rouge of it, like an apple amongst the creaminess of her complexion, looked lush and kissable. Her eyelashes fell lightly against her cheeks. Her wild wavy hair framing the lot as if she'd just been painted by Rubens himself.

He found himself wishing for his camera again. Wanting to capture the way the gentle morning light enhanced her too wide eyes and her too big mouth into something quite striking.

Wondering if that too big mouth of hers kissed as well as it wisecracked.

If it was as good a lover as it was a talker.

A louder engine roared in the distance just as things beneath the covers started to stir, snapping Kent out of his stupor.

What the hell was he doing?

He sat bolt upright, displacing her hand and waking her in the process.

'Come on, Sadie Bliss,' he said briskly as he kicked out

of his swag. 'The day has started and I'm starving.' He ignored her groan. 'Let's hustle.'

An hour later, Sadie left Kent to another disgustingly unhealthy roadhouse breakfast as she headed for the amenities. Yes, she was starving, but she was seeing Leo today and she was doing that with the flattest stomach possible even if it meant depriving herself of food all day.

Plus she needed a shower. Badly.

The facilities were fairly basic and she thanked God she'd thought to bring her own shampoo and conditioner. Her hair was thick and did not take kindly to cheap products.

Still, even with hair products that cost a small fortune, Sadie despaired as she looked into the grimy mirror. She sucked in her cheeks in the vain hope that they'd look like they used to—all hollowed and model-like. She hunched her shoulders to enhance her collarbones. She pirouetted and craned her neck around to try and see if the size of her bum had reduced any in the last few days.

Even the minimiser bra she'd bought especially didn't seem to look as good in the cheap roadhouse lights as it had in the expensive Sydney department store.

If only she'd known about this trip a month ago—she could have at least done something earlier.

She'd spent a lot of the last few years imagining her first meeting with Leo again. How she would look, what she would say, how he would react. And she could already sense the reality and fantasy were hopelessly mismatched.

She'd wanted Leo to weep when he saw her. To rue the day he'd told her to go. To eat his words. Words that had struck right at her very core.

Who's going to want you, Sadie? You're nothing without me.

And she'd wanted to be smoking hot when he did.

She didn't care how vain, how girly that made her. How much it didn't make sense. Leo had worshipped her body, had immortalised it in dozens of his works, and she wanted to show him that she still had it.

That Sadie Bliss was wanted plenty.

She screwed up her nose at her reflection. Could she pull it off?

And what would she do if he crooked that imperious little finger at her? Because despite everything there was still a damaged part of her, the Daddy's girl, that craved his approval.

Sadie dialled the number Tabitha had given her as she made her way across to Kent, who was filling up the vehicle. Her heart was pounding in her chest as it rang in her ear and when it picked up her pulse spiked so quickly she thought she was going to faint.

Which turned out to be unnecessary given that it was Leo's PA who answered the phone. Kevin informed her Leo was painting and not to be disturbed, but that he would pass on the message that the *Sunday On My Mind* reporter was expected by mid afternoon.

'Is that *Leo*?' Kent asked as he returned to the vehicle after paying for the fuel.

She ignored his childish emphasis. 'They're expecting us.'

'Ready to go?'

Sadie nodded absently. As ready as she was ever going to be. No time now for losing some last-minute pounds.

This was the day.

'Your cup of tea is in the dashboard cup-holder,' he said as he swung up into the vehicle.

Sadie buckled up and they got under way. She sipped

her tea and ignored her growling stomach and the light-headed feeling making her a little dizzy. She watched out of the window as the flat red earth and occasional scrubby bushland passed by in a blur, her mind preoccupied with seeing Leo again after three years.

Her enthusiasm of the last forty-eight hours to get Kent talking was non-existent today. She didn't even notice the jolts and rattles of the vehicle as it negotiated the far more potholed highway. Her mind was busy and her gut was gradually screwing itself into a tighter and tighter ball.

Kent, however, did notice the jolting and the shaking, particularly in the interesting way it manifested itself. Sadie's chest shifted and bounced in his peripheral vision, totally screwing with his concentration. His initial relief that she wasn't going to be Little Miss Nosey was quickly tempered. At least conversation might have kept his mind on something other than the way her breasts rocked and swayed in rhythm with the vehicle.

After two hours of complete silence from her, Kent couldn't stand it for another moment. Particularly when she was wound as tight as a bow string and frowning enough to give her wrinkles that no amount of youth serum would fix. Her thoughts were so loud he could almost hear them forming.

He gave a slight shake of his head as he opened his mouth to speak, not quite believing that he was the one initiating conversation. 'Penny for them?' he asked.

Sadie frowned as she turned towards his voice. It took a second for his question to register front and centre in her brain. 'Nothing,' she dismissed. 'Just…formulating some questions for the interview.'

'Then why are you frowning so much. He doesn't bite, does he?'

Sadie didn't answer as she thought about Leo's particular brand of scathing wit. Plenty of people had felt the sting of it. He wasn't a man who tolerated fools very gladly.

It was Kent's turn to frown at her silence. 'Does he?' he demanded. Photographing celebrities already felt like a sell-out. He wasn't going to pander to an overinflated ego, no matter how well regarded he was in the art world.

Sadie frowned again. 'What? Oh…no, he doesn't bite.'

Kent cocked an eyebrow. 'So you do know him?'

Sadie pulled her gaze away from the probing reach of his. 'How much longer do you think?'

Kent stood waiting at a petrol station in Borroloola his good foot resting up on the bull bar, a map spread over the red-dust-encrusted bonnet of his vehicle, studying the directions to Leonard Pinto's outback retreat. Sadie had insisted on stopping here even though they'd not long stopped at a roadhouse for lunch.

Well, at least he'd eaten lunch. She'd nibbled on a small apple and hadn't even finished it. But given her little speech from day one about her cast-iron bladder he was surprised she needed to use the bathroom again so soon.

Movement to his left snagged his attention and he turned his head to focus on the woman walking towards him. It took him a beat or two to realise it was Sadie.

He blinked.

She was wearing a dress. A flowing red dress with shoestring straps that showed the tiniest hint of cleavage. It outlined her thighs and fell in a fringed hem just below her knees.

It was hardly revealing, in fact it seemed to just skim everything. To hint but not reveal.

But the way it flowed against her body, moved against her curves, the way the red offset her hair and complemented her mouth and skin was nothing short of a marvel.

She drew level with him and asked, 'Does this look okay?'

Okay?

Kent felt as if he had a few short days ago in Tabitha's office—as if his eyes were poking out on springs. Up close he could see she'd enhanced her eyes a little with some dark kohl, had smeared some gloss on her mouth, big silver hoops hung from her ear lobes. Her raven hair flowed around her shoulders.

She looked like a gypsy and Kent struggled to keep himself from falling under her spell.

'Wow,' was about all he could manage when he realised he hadn't answered her hesitant enquiry. But it seemed to do the trick as a huge grin kicked her crazy big mouth up at the sides.

'Right answer,' she murmured. 'For a moment I thought you were going to say fine.'

He shrugged. 'I *was* toying with mighty fine.'

'Ah,' she smiled. 'You're learning.'

He smiled back. 'I didn't know we had to dress?'

'Just trying to make a good impression,' she quipped as she moved past him to the passenger seat, feeling more confident from Kent's positive reaction.

Kent blinked again. 'That ought to do it,' he muttered under his breath.

He started up the car and pulled out onto the road. The cab was full of a new fragrance. Gone was the smell of earth, diesel fumes, aged leather and axle grease. It smelled like passionfruit and something headier, something that reminded him of sex, and he doubted he'd ever get the aroma out of the upholstery.

Out of his head.

And it irritated him. Largely because he realised he'd

spent three whole days not thinking about having sex with Sadie Bliss and now that was all he *could* think about!

Somehow, in such a short time, her smart pouty mouth and treacherous curves had managed to get under his skin.

In his peripheral vision he could see her foot tapping briskly on the floor. Or rather he could see the ripple effects as it vibrated through her thigh and wobbled through her chest.

A thigh and chest he suddenly wished he knew a hell of a lot better.

Damn it. Sadie should have flown. She should have insisted. *He should have insisted.*

Damn Tabitha Fox to hell!

'You seem nervous,' he said, because if he had to watch anything more shift on Sadie Bliss he was going to be the one to make it so.

Sadie jiggled her leg. 'I am.'

'First big interview?'

Sadie shook her head. 'No. I mean yes. It's my first big interview but that's not why I'm nervous.'

'Oh?' Kent continued, pleased to see she'd stopped her infernal jiggling.

Sadie looked at Kent, his eyes fixed on the road, his beautiful mouth a perfect slash in his perfect profile. She was so nervous she wanted to throw up.

So nervous she couldn't keep it to herself any longer. The need to share the burden of it all was upon her suddenly like a big black cloud.

'Leo and I used to be lovers.'

CHAPTER SIX

KENT was so stunned by the admission he didn't see another massive pothole until they hit it and they both bounced in their seats as the whole cab rattled and shook. He'd suspected from the beginning she knew Pinto somehow and her *Leo* slip had confirmed it, but never in a million years would he have thought this.

Sadie glanced at Kent as he drove along without a word. *Back to the strong silent type again.* Not something she needed right now. She needed someone to give her a pep talk. To tell her that what happened in the past didn't matter. The clock had been reset and she would be fine.

God, anything would do, anything at all.

She just needed him to say *something*.

'Nothing to say?' she demanded after his continuing silence stretched her nerves to their limit.

Kent glanced at her, his brain still grappling with the bombshell. The number of questions he had probably outnumbered the stars in last night's sky but he wasn't going to get into this with her.

He looked back at the road. What she did with her life was her own concern. It was absolutely nothing to do with him.

He'd known her for three days and it didn't matter that she was sitting in his car in a dress that oozed sex or that he wanted to pull over and have his way with her because that was never going to happen. They were doing a job together and when it was done they'd probably never see each other again.

So, she had a thing for older guys. If she wanted to sleep with men twenty years her senior then good luck to her.

Or to them anyway.

'None of my business,' he said, trying not to think about the twelve years that separated them.

Sadie glared at him. Kent's lack of enquiry drove her nuts. She'd spent the last three days foraging for crumbs from him thinking it was just about his privacy, but maybe it was really that he didn't give a damn about anyone else?

'That's it? That's all you've got?'

Kent shrugged. 'Who you've slept with is nothing to do with me.'

'What, no, isn't he a little old for you, Sadie Bliss? Or, how the hell did that come about, Sadie Bliss?'

Kent sighed. Sadie obviously wanted to talk about it and, as much as he didn't want to know any more about her, there was a part of him that really, really wanted to know how a smoking-hot woman like Sadie ended up with a guy twice her age.

If Leonard Pinto had been buff and handsome he might have been able to see it, but Kent had seen the man's picture and he doubted good old Leo would ever be asked to pose for a centrefold.

'Okay, then, out with it,' he said. 'You obviously want to get it off your chest, so spill.'

Sadie looked out of the window, not in the mood to be humoured. 'It doesn't matter.'

Kent glanced at her petulant profile and felt as if he were back in high school. 'I'm not going to ask you twice, Sadie, so why don't you tell me all about it? Tell me how a man who must be at least twenty years older than you came to be in a sexual relationship with a much younger woman.'

Sadie turned to face him, her eyes blazing. 'It wasn't like that.'

Kent raised an eyebrow. 'Like what?'

'The way you're making it sound,' she snapped.

'Okay. So how was it, then?'

Sadie turned back to the window, watching the scenery flash by as she gathered her thoughts. 'I took one of his classes at art school.'

Kent snorted. If Sadie thought that made things sound better, then she was much more immature than he'd originally thought.

'So…he was your teacher? Isn't that against the rules?'

Sadie sent him a scathing look. 'I took the class for a term. We didn't get involved until six months later.'

'And how did that start? No, let me guess. He was impressed with your talent and offered to give you extra tuition.'

Sadie looked back out of the window. 'I went to one of his exhibitions and we got talking. He took me out for drinks afterwards.'

'And then he said come back to my place and take off your clothes, I want to paint you?'

Sadie ignored the sarcasm. 'He was the most articulate and witty man I'd ever met. Sophisticated. Urbane. And what he didn't know about the world and art and culture wasn't worth knowing. And he was interested in me. This older, interesting man who could have had his pick of women was interested in little ol' me.'

Kent frowned. Obviously her father's desertion had had a lasting impact on Sadie. 'Why wouldn't he be? You're an interesting person.'

Not to mention how very interesting she was to look at.

Sadie flicked him an *oh-really* look. 'Yes, I've noticed how you've been completely enthralled by my life.'

Kent shrugged. 'Don't take it personally. I've been pretty uninterested generally the last couple of years.' He swerved to avoid another crater-like pothole, then looked at her. 'I can't believe, though, that there weren't a veritable glut of men your age that were also interested?'

She nodded. 'Sure. In my E cups.' Sadie looked back out of the window. 'Guys my age tend to have conversations with my chest. Leonard didn't. He looked me right in the eye.'

Kent felt an instant spike of guilt at his own fascination with her chest, but at least he could take comfort from the fact that *every* part of her seemed to fascinate him.

God knew her mouth was becoming an obsession.

'So Leonard's gay? Or bi, I guess.'

Sadie gasped and turned to stare at him. Where in the hell had that come from? 'Were you dropped on the head as a baby?'

'Hey, nothing wrong with that,' Kent assured her. He could understand Sadie being attracted to someone who didn't objectify her. 'I'm just saying that any man who doesn't at least check you out can't be heterosexual.'

Sadie opened her mouth to blast him despite the traitorous part of her that felt curiously flattered. 'Are you implying that *all* men aren't capable of restraining Neanderthal behaviour and if they are then they must be gay?'

'Heterosexual men check out women, Sadie.' He shrugged. 'I agree it's appalling that some guys behave like morons and that subtlety isn't part of their repertoire, but we're pretty simple creatures really, genetically predisposed to appreciate the female form. It's just as natural as breathing.'

Sadie wondered for a moment if Kent had checked her

out. In *that* way. And if so, when? She hadn't really noticed him gawking like the average male and he'd certainly
never had one of those conversations with her breasts that
annoyed her so much. In fact she'd have to say that Kent
had displayed supreme lack of interest.

Annoyed at the direction of her thoughts when her mind
needed to be on Leo, Sadie grappled to get back on the
page. 'Trust me, he's straight,' she said icily, seeking and
holding his gaze for a moment. 'Very, very straight. We
had lots and lots and lots of sex.'

Which wasn't exactly true. Leonard had been more into
oral sex and they'd had plenty of that but he'd not been
great at reciprocating. Still, he'd stimulated her in other
ways, intellectually and artistically, so his low sex drive
hadn't ever been an issue.

Being his lover had transcended the physical.

Kent dragged his gaze back to the road as her doe eyes
told him stuff he wasn't sure he was keen on knowing. He
really did not want to be regaled with stories of Leonard
Pinto's straightness.

Not as it pertained to Sadie anyway.

'So *did* he paint you?' he said, trying to shift the conversation.

Sadie nodded. 'Oh, yes. I became his muse. Gave up art
school, moved in with him so I could pose for him whenever he wanted. All hours of the day or night. It was…
exhilarating.'

And it had been. His obsession with her had been heady
stuff. It had also been exhausting. Living with an arty
temperament had its downside, especially when she was
struggling to find time for her own art.

Still, she'd have never taken that part of her life back.

'He didn't paint anyone else for nearly two years.'

Kent heard pride soften her voice. It sounded a little

co-dependent to him, but Kent couldn't blame the guy and a part of him hoped he might get to see one of those paintings.

He remembered wanting to photograph her this morning and, whilst he wasn't a fan of Pinto's nudes, Kent couldn't deny he was curious to see a master's take on Sadie's curvy perfection. Had Leonard managed to capture the perfectness of her imperfect features?

Although quite how Pinto managed to be so productive with Sadie living in his house and stripped naked a lot of the time he had no clue. He knew for damn sure there wouldn't be a lot of work going on if she was buck naked and posing for him!

His groin stirred and he clamped down on unproductive thoughts as he zeroed in on the most startling part of her story. 'You gave up art school?'

Sadie nodded. She'd cut herself off from everything, even her mother. Completely isolated herself. Weeks would go by without seeing another soul and she'd revelled in it, satisfied with being the centre of Leo's world, buying in to his control over her because she'd loved him and believed he loved her.

'I was never really good anyway,' she dismissed.

Kent blinked. That was the second time she'd written off her ability. 'Says who?' Art schools were notoriously difficult to get into—they only took talented students. It had taken him two years of applying before he'd been accepted into one to study photography.

'Leo.'

'And you believed him?'

Sadie rolled her eyes. 'He's Leonard Pinto. I think he knows a thing or two about talent, don't you?'

Kent thought good old Leo also knew a thing or two

about manipulation. 'How old were you when you hooked up with Pinto?'

'Nineteen,' she said wistfully.

Kent paused as that info sank in. 'And he was?'

'Thirty-nine.'

Oh, yeah. *Leo knew which side his bread was buttered on.*

'What happened?' Kent asked. 'How'd it end?'

'Behind my back my mother gathered a portfolio of my work and put me up for a scholarship to my dream college in London. And I got it.'

Kent shook his head. And she *still* believed she didn't have any talent? 'I'm guessing Leonard was none too pleased to have his muse running away.'

Sadie looked away. 'I hadn't painted in over a year. Leo loved me, he didn't want me to fail. He was right to point out that I'd lost my edge. That I wouldn't last long there, that places like that require exceptional talent and dedication. That I'd probably only got in because of my association with him.'

Kent ground his teeth at Pinto's disingenuous actions. *Nice.* 'So you didn't want to go?'

Sadie shook her head. 'No. I did want to go. I'd been doing nothing for a year and I was getting restless. I just...'

'What?'

'It was hard. Leo saw it as a betrayal.'

Kent snorted. 'I thought he loved you.'

Sadie looked away. No. That had been her mistake. She had loved him. Leo had never loved her. 'I was torn and he told me the decision should be easy and as it wasn't that I should go.'

Kent didn't know what to say. Pinto sounded like a total arse. 'Did you go to London?'

Sadie shook her head, she'd been devastated by the

whole thing. 'I needed to get away from art for a while. So I studied journalism instead. And here I am today coming full circle.'

'So, why does Pinto want you for the interview?'

Sadie shrugged. 'Curiosity probably. I think he thought I would fall apart without him. Whatever his agenda is, I'm determined to show him I didn't.'

Kent looked at her, then looked away. 'Well, that dress ought to do it.'

He slowed as he saw the sign for Casa Del Leone, the Pinto retreat, approaching, but not before he noticed that fabulous mouth break into a broad grin.

Neither of them spoke as they drove into the property. The house, complete with massive marble columns, looked as if it had been picked up from Ancient Greece and deposited by Zeus himself. It looked completely out of place in the middle of the Australian outback.

Kent whistled as he pulled the vehicle into the Grecian portico. 'It looks like a pimple on a pumpkin,' Kent said as he reached for his seat belt.

'Wait,' Sadie said, putting her hand on his forearm.

Kent frowned at her. 'What?'

Sadie looked at the imposing marble entryway and massive wrought-iron door, her heart suddenly pounding loud enough to shake the columns to their foundations. 'Do not let me get sucked in by him, okay?'

Kent's frown deepened as he looked at her hand on his arm. 'Please tell me after everything you've just told me, you're not still in love with him.'

Sadie shook her head. 'No…I don't think so.' Kent's impatient look spurred her to clarification. 'He was a big part of my life for a long time. He was like…an addiction or something. And addicts are never really cured, are they?'

She chewed on her bottom lip. 'I'm afraid I'm going to get a taste and...fall off the wagon.'

Kent's gaze involuntarily followed the action of her teeth as they ate away her lip gloss. When he realised he was staring he dropped his gaze to her revenge attire. 'I think you're stronger than you think, Sadie Bliss.'

Sadie smiled at him, suddenly conscious of the warmth of him beneath her palm and the bunch of muscles in his forearm. She was surprised how good they felt. How the power of them did funny things to her insides.

He was so different from Leo. And not just in looks. Leo would never have calmly told her she was strong.

Leo had spent two years telling her she needed him.

'Come on,' he said briskly, because she was looking at him with those big doe eyes and the ridiculous urge to lean over and kiss her was growing stronger.

Neither of them needed that. Not now.

Not ever.

He undid his belt, her hand falling away. 'Let's do this thing.'

Leonard's PA greeted them at the door. 'Mr Pinto is in his studio and is not to be disturbed for another two hours. I'll show you to your rooms and then take you on a tour,' he said.

They spent the next two hours touring around the palatial house and grounds. Kent dutifully took photographs and Sadie asked all the standard questions. It was late afternoon when they were invited to *freshen up* and join *Mr Pinto* for pre-dinner drinks at six in the *saloon*.

Kent felt as if he'd just walked into the set of an Agatha Christie movie but he did as he was told, having a shower and getting changed into clean jeans and a casual skivvy.

He took his camera with him as he headed for the *Gone With The Wind* staircase.

Sadie, who was still in her killer dress, met him at the top and they descended together. 'I feel like I should be calling you Scarlett,' he murmured.

Sadie laughed. 'Why, Rhett, I do declare...'

Kevin fixed them both a drink and they all made polite conversation whilst they waited for the guest of honour. Leo turned up twenty-five minutes later.

'Sadie!' he exclaimed from the doorway.

Sadie, who had been chatting to Kevin, rose to her feet, her heart pounding again as the man she'd once loved walked briskly towards her.

'Leo,' she murmured as he swept her into a hug.

Sadie shut her eyes and waited for the familiar intoxicating rush she'd always experienced just from his presence. When it didn't come she opened them to find herself looking directly into Kent's gaze. He was standing near the large floor-to-ceiling French doors across the other side of the room in her direct line of sight.

He winked at her and she found herself suppressing a smile as Leo held her for a little longer than she was comfortable with.

'My goodness,' Leo said as he finally released her and held her away at arm's length. 'I think you've been living the high life. Where have all those lovely bones gone, darling?'

Kent watched Sadie's smile falter and before he knew it he was striding towards them. The urge to punch Leonard Pinto in the face was one he was just able to suppress as he stuck out his hand and introduced himself.

'Ah, yes, Mr Nelson,' Leo said, grasping Kent's hand. 'Kevin mentioned that you were the photographer. It is indeed a great pleasure to meet you.'

Kent nodded. He supposed he should have returned the compliment, but Sadie's smile in his peripheral vision was so brittle he thought it might actually crumble off her face and, frankly, Leonard Pinto's handshake had been unimpressive.

Kevin handed Leo his standard gin and tonic and regaled Kent with his attempts at photography. Sadie listened to them on autopilot. She'd nibbled on an apple all day and the glass of white wine she was sipping was going straight to her head.

She tried not to let Leo's opening comment get to her—he'd never been a particularly sensitive man—but she'd starved herself for days and knew she looked damn good. Not rake thin as she had been, but good nonetheless.

Would it have killed him to have given her a compliment?

Leo laughed at a joke he'd told and Sadie ran her eyes over him. He hadn't changed. Maybe there was a little more grey in the wings at his temple, some more padding under his chin and around his middle, but he was the same. Tall and thin, with long arty fingers, curiously not paint stained as per usual, and bookish wire-rimmed glasses.

She waited for the rush of tangled emotions he'd always aroused and was relieved to feel nothing.

She switched her attention to Kent and his polite fixed smile. The comparison between the two men was striking. Kent was toned and broad and fit-looking compared to Leo's obvious indoor physique. Kent's spare, angular features were sharply contrasted with the gentle planes of Leo's.

Sadie had never placed any stead on looks but with the two of them together it was hard not to compare. Kent looked like a Rodin sculpture—all symmetry and fluid lines. Leo looked like a kindergarten art project—something that you cherished because of an association but not something you wanted to just look at for hours.

'The evening meal is served,' Kevin announced interrupting Sadie's reverie.

Kent watched Sadie nibble pathetically around the edges of her meal. It was all beautifully cooked by Kevin who seemed to be general dogsbody, but it just wasn't his thing.

Small servings, big plates, posh names.

By the end of it Kent was still starving.

And Sadie must have been ready to eat the table leg.

More polite conversation was made about the local area and the history of the house until Kevin took away the last plate.

'Would you like a tour of the studio now?' Leonard asked them as he stood.

Kent looked at Sadie, a half-query in his eyes. Personally he'd rather drive to the nearest steak restaurant and order the biggest Waygu they had.

'Sure,' Sadie said, standing also, her head spinning a little. She was curious to see what kind of space he painted in now, in this marble mausoleum in the middle of nowhere.

Leo, ever the charming host, regaled them with stories as he led the way towards the back of the house. He opened a large double wooden door, flicking a light on in the darkened room illuminating the space inside and out.

The first thing she noticed was that the studio overlooked the man-made lake Kevin had shown them earlier. The next was how clean it was. She knew Leo, she knew him well, and when he was in the middle of a project—the studio was always a shambles.

The third thing she only noticed when Kent said, 'Holy cow.' She turned to look up on the wall behind her to see what had his jaw dropping.

A giant nude portrait hung there. Of her. And for a moment all three of them just stood and looked at it.

'My best, don't you think, Sadie?'

Sadie nodded as she remembered how many hours she'd sat for this particular painting. She felt her cheeks flush as Kent's gaze continually darted over it. It wasn't the same as seeing her naked in the flesh, she knew, but it was still her up there, lying reclined in all her glory.

Kent couldn't believe what he was seeing. He'd hoped to see something like this. To see a true artist capture Sadie's likeness. But this portrait was shocking. The Sadie in the painting was a far cry from the woman he'd shared a car with for the last few days.

She was very thin. Her bones stuck out, her curves were non-existent and her breasts were much smaller.

He looked down at her, horrified. 'My God, were you ill?' he asked.

Leo blanched at Kent's blunt question. 'I beg your pardon,' he blustered. 'She was much healthier then. Look at that bone structure. Those angles. She's the very picture of female beauty, of what men desire in women. And she worked hard to look that good, didn't you, darling?'

Kent looked at Leo Pinto as if he'd just grown another head. Suddenly Sadie's eating patterns of the last few days, her '*It's complicated*,' made sense.

Leo had obviously been starving her for two years.

And facing him again as a successful, independent career woman must have taken a lot of courage.

Finally he understood her. Understood the celery sticks and the oversized T-shirts.

And he understood why. Leo Pinto.

She'd loved him to the point that she'd become someone else for him.

And he'd let her.

Toxic bastard.

He looked at a silent Sadie, then back at the painting. He hated it on sight. She looked like his ballerina nudes.

Thin and androgynous.

She did not look like Sadie Bliss.

'I'm sorry, Mr Pinto,' Kevin interrupted from the doorway, a phone in his hand. 'It's your agent—he says it's urgent.'

Leo gave Kent a pained smile and ran his fingers down the back of Sadie's arm. 'I won't be a moment.'

Kent watched him go, then turned back to Sadie. She was looking at the painting with an inscrutable expression and he couldn't figure out whether it was admiration, indifference or revulsion.

'Are you okay?' he asked.

Sadie nodded absently, rubbing her arms, feeling suddenly cold and very light-headed. It had been interesting seeing the portrait again with time and distance on her side.

Interesting to see it through Kent's eyes too.

'You've been starving yourself to look like that?' he asked incredulously, jabbing a finger in the general direction of the portrait. 'You don't seriously believe that men find bones and angles attractive, do you?'

'I used to,' she said. 'Leo used to say I had the perfect face on the wrong body but that could be fixed.' Spots started to swim before her eyes as she dragged her gaze away from the portrait she'd once loved so much.

Kent watched as Sadie swayed and he grabbed her upper arms in alarm. 'You're not okay.'

Sadie nodded as his strong, frowning face swam before her eyes. 'Just a little light-headed,' she dismissed, but reached for his arms for extra anchorage.

'I'm not surprised. That's what happens when you don't eat anything. Come on, I have a Mars bar in my bag.'

Something told him there wouldn't be anything so common in *Casa Del Idiot*.

'No,' she resisted. 'Just give me a moment. It'll pass.'

Kent shook his head as he looked back at the painting. The woman staring back at him looked utterly miserable. Thin for sure, but where was the vibrant woman of sass and spark he'd come to know the past few days? 'That is a tragedy,' he muttered.

'Thanks a lot,' Sadie half joked, looking up into his face. He was still holding her, his scratchy-looking jaw line in profile. 'I was rather fond of my bony look.'

Kent looked down at her in alarm. Which was a mistake, because her mouth was so very, very near, her red dress like a beacon in his peripheral vision. That passion-fruit smell enveloped him in a flurry of very bad ideas. He dropped his gaze to the plump pillows turned up towards him, thinking that thin was never a good look.

Not on bodies. Or mouths. 'Trust me, curvy looks way better.'

Sadie could feel the heat of his gaze on her mouth. She shifted her hands so they were lying more comfortably against his biceps. 'Leo always said that men lied about liking curves, that given a choice they'd choose skinny every time.'

Kent frowned. 'God, he's a pretentious arse.'

Sadie smiled, but Leo's words still stung after all these years. She traced a finger absently around the bulk of a bicep. 'He said no one would ever want me.'

Kent shook his head as her doe eyes blinked up at him. His pulse was pounding through his ears as her body swayed closer to his. He swallowed as desire bolted through his system. He shouldn't kiss her. Not in a client's house. And certainly not standing under a life-sized image of her in the buff. But she smelled so damn good and her lips were so damn near. Nearer as he moved his face closer to hers.

'He's wrong,' Kent muttered.

Sadie's breath quickened as his lips descended. She hung onto his words. Looking at her portrait again, listening to Leo's rapture over it had sucked her back into a turbulent time in her life, but this man—this potent virile he-man, the polar opposite to Leo in every way—was telling her something different.

He was going to kiss her in this room, in front of that painting.

And she needed it. She needed to be desired for the person she was now, not the one she'd been.

The air crackled around them as their lips met. Kent felt no resistance, just her body completely aligning with his and her incredible mouth opening to him on a little whimper that reached right inside his gut and squeezed.

And then it was gone as a much hotter, deeper, more urgent need consumed him. The need to claim, to conquer, to lead. He sucked in a breath, pushing his hands into her hair and his tongue into her mouth, feeling the tentative touch of hers grow bolder.

But then voices getting nearer started to intrude and Kent suddenly realised where he was. He pulled away, her little disappointed mew and moist pouty mouth almost bringing him to his knees.

'You okay?' he asked, when she opened her big grey eyes, now the colour of slate, his arms steadying her.

Sadie blinked and nodded as she heard Leo enter the room even though she wasn't sure she'd ever be okay again.

CHAPTER SEVEN

THE kiss kept Sadie awake long into the night. Nothing kept Sadie awake long into the night. Especially not something that probably didn't even last twenty seconds. It was practically over before it began but, man, did it have an impact!

It had certainly shot her flagging blood sugar into the stratosphere. And as she lay in the dark staring at the ceiling she felt as if she were still riding the sugar high.

It had been impossible to concentrate on Leo after the impulsive kiss. All she'd been aware of was the tingle in her lips, the fizz in her blood and Kent's brooding monosyllabic presence nearby. Had he felt as flummoxed as she had? Or was it just another gallant deed *he-men* performed every day for damsels in distress?

The kiss of life to revive flagging blood sugars and dented egos.

She had escaped as soon as possible to get away from Kent. To get away from both of them.

Two very different men who had both rocked her world.

Kent hadn't attempted to stop her or even follow, for which she was grateful. She needed some distance. To gain some perspective. Like the perspective she'd gained over Leo since being apart from him for the last few years.

Because she seriously doubted that one little kiss meant anything to Kent, especially considering how very hard he'd tried to have absolutely nothing to do with her the entire trip.

Men flirted with her. It was just a fact of her life no matter how hard she dressed down and didn't try to draw attention to herself.

But not Kent. Kent had been blunt in his complete lack of interest.

Which only made the kiss more puzzling.

But it had been an odd moment. And straight afterwards he had looked as if he were contemplating hacking his lips off. Reading something into it would be a bad idea. It would be something the nineteen-year-old Sadie would have done. Latching onto anyone who flattered her and showed an interest in anything other than the contents of her bra.

Twenty-four-year-old Sadie used her head.

And it was telling her to get a grip.

After her restless night Sadie woke late. Kevin informed her that Kent had headed out about midnight to take photographs and wasn't expected back until after lunch. And that Mr Pinto would receive her in his studio at ten.

Sadie felt an immediate sense of loss. The memory of her starry night on top of Kent's Land Rover had stayed with her and the pull to see an outback night again, to see it as he saw it, through a lens, was undeniable.

And what was she supposed to read into his sudden walkabout? Was it his not-so-subtle way of saying that he didn't want to talk about what had happened?

That the kiss hadn't meant anything?

That it had been a mistake?

'Egg-white omelette?'

Kevin's question broke into her swirling thoughts. She

shook her head, her hunger pangs dampened by her confusion. 'Just a cup of tea, please.'

Twenty minutes later she was knocking on Leo's studio door in a similar shoestring-strapped dress to yesterday, hinting and skimming in a deep ochre like the colour of the earth outside the oasis that Leo had built for himself. It buttoned all the way up the front with tiny black buttons. Her hair was clasped behind in a tight ponytail. Strappy sandals adorned her feet. Dark kohl emphasised her eyes and gloss drew attention to her mouth.

It had been tempting to interview him in her travel clothes just to see that annoyed little crease he got between his brows. But she was a professional and she was working, representing *Sunday On My Mind,* and she wouldn't compromise that.

And, in Leo's presence, her career was like a shield against his poisonous words from the past, so she was going to armour herself in the full uniform and hold her head up high.

Leo pulled the door open. 'Sadie!'

He pulled her towards him into an embrace, kissing her on the mouth before Sadie could take evasive action and lingering a little longer than was polite. She pulled back and noticed a fleeting look of confusion on his face before he ushered her in.

Light filled the room from the large windows and Sadie was struck again by how clean the studio was. She looked around for half-finished canvases stacked against the walls, drop sheets, preliminary sketches littering the ample bench tops. Even the familiar toxic chemical odour of paint, so inherent in his studio, was strangely absent.

'I've never seen your studio so sparkling before,' she remarked.

Leo shrugged. 'I've never allowed a photographer into

my space before,' he said, indicating the studio looking even more cavernous with the usual chaos cleaned away. 'Can't have the public knowing what a pigsty I work in.'

Sadie noticed his very clean-looking hands again. The entire two years she'd lived with him Leo's fingers had rarely been without paint stains. 'Are you between projects at the moment?'

Leo nodded briskly. 'I've set up some chairs over by the windows,' he said, moving towards them. 'Will that be okay for the interview?'

Sadie followed him over to the two low bucket chairs separated by a coffee table upon which there was a carafe of water and two glasses. Kevin appeared as she sat down, handing Leo his usual gin and tonic, and enquired as to whether she wanted something else to drink. She declined and he poured her some water as she rummaged through her bag for her notebook and her tape recorder.

'Do you mind?' she asked as she set it on the table between them.

Leo shook his head. 'Not at all.'

Sadie felt ridiculously nervous as she started the interview. She knew the man intimately and it was hardly her first job, but she didn't want to stuff it up. Leo had told her she couldn't make it without him and it was imperative to prove she could.

She had.

Two hours later it was over and Sadie was exhausted from the polite pretence between them. Especially with Leo's continual efforts to sabotage Sadie's professionalism by spicing his answers with personal details of their past life together. Her nerves were at screeching point when she closed her notebook and pronounced herself satisfied.

Leo stretched back in the chair and looked at her for long moments. 'What are you doing, Sadie?'

Sadie contemplated pretending she didn't know what he was asking, but decided that playing coy wasn't her style any more. 'I'm doing my job,' she said as she stuffed the tools of her trade back in her handbag.

Leo stood and held out his hand to her. 'Come,' he commanded.

Sadie looked up at his outstretched hand and cocked an eyebrow at him. 'I beg your pardon?'

Leo sighed. 'Let me show you something.'

After a moment or two Sadie stood ignoring his hand. She let him usher her over, his hand at her elbow, to stand in the middle of the room facing the painting of her. Neither of them said anything for a moment.

'You belong here with me.'

Sadie felt the pull, the allure, of the painting even after all this time. Every brushstroke told a story of a time in her life when she'd been deliriously happy. When a man had cosseted her and celebrated her female form instead of lamenting it as her father had done.

'Look how beautiful you are,' Leo whispered.

His finger stroked the inside of her elbow and tears blurred in Sadie's eyes—she had looked good. But being back here with him beside her she also remembered his obsession with her body. And how she'd bought into it. As her stomach rumbled again she remembered those days when she would have killed for a cheeseburger and fries.

When not even his compliments could soothe the ache that continually gnawed at her gut.

When the diet pills and the caffeine and nights of no sleep as Leo painted her obsessively had left her strung out.

With distance she could recognise the insanity of it.

'I could help you get back to that, Sadie. Stay here with me. Let me paint you again.'

His voice was low and, oh, so familiar as his thumb

continued to stroke her arm. Sadie fought against the illicit thrill of addiction. She shook her head. 'I have another job now.'

'I bet it doesn't measure up to being Leonard Pinto's muse. I need you, Sadie. We need each other.'

It was his utter arrogance that helped pull her back from the edge. A few years ago she'd revelled in that title; now it turned her stomach.

He might as well have said Leonard Pinto's plaything.

As if she were some doll he could manipulate into whatever position he wanted.

She looked down at his thumb still stroking her. The skin was pink as a newborn babe's and she could see the whorl of his fingerprint. *I need you, Sadie.*

She took a step away from him as realisation dawned, his hand falling away. 'Oh, my God. You're blocked, aren't you?' She looked around at the studio gleaming like a luxury car showroom. 'You're not in between projects at all.'

Leo looked at the floor. 'A small slump,' he dismissed.

'How long, Leo?' she asked his downcast head.

When he finally looked at her again she could tell he was steeling himself to lie. But then his shoulders sagged and he looked significantly more than twenty years her senior. 'I haven't painted anything decent since you left.'

Sadie blinked at his admission. She'd been gone for over three years. *That had to be killing him.*

Leo looked at her. 'You belong here with me, Sadie.'

He sounded like a petulant child and Sadie shook her head as she realised she was finally free of him. 'No. I belong to me. And I have a job that I love.'

'You *loved* posing for me.'

His interjection was almost a whine and she took pity on him. 'It's not a real career, Leo.'

'That didn't seem to bother you at the time.'

Sadie ignored his sarcasm and the truth of it. 'Journalism can take me places. I've been out for just a few months and already I have a shot at my dream job.'

Leo stuck his hand on his hip. 'Thanks to me. You've only got this shot because you slept with *me*. I warned you—you were nothing without me.'

Sadie reeled a little as the crudeness of his triumphant accusation sank in. He'd obviously been waiting three years to throw that one in her face. And it was true—she had scored this interview because of her association with Leo. But she wasn't the lost young woman he'd tossed away a few years back—she had a spine these days and his slights didn't have the power to hurt any more.

She certainly wasn't going to hang around listening to any more. 'Goodbye, Leo,' she said, turning away from him.

'Sadie, wait!'

She contemplated ignoring him, but the urgency in his voice pulled her up and she turned around.

'You walk away and you're walking away from that.' He pointed to the painting. 'You'll never get a shot at being her again.'

Sadie looked at the painting and finally saw what Kent had seen last night. Bones and angles and hollows. Leo had even painted her breasts smaller—artistic licence, as he was so fond of quoting. Suddenly she looked like just another skinny Hollywood starlet or skeletal model.

Like every ballerina he'd ever painted.

It didn't look like her.

'I don't want to be her, Leo. I like me. I like the me I am now.'

She stalled for a moment, realising the words that had just fallen out were utterly true. Time, distance and Kent's kiss had put some things into perspective.

'I like to eat good food and drink good wine and I love junk food as well! I like those little tiny marshmallows on my cornflakes for breakfast and hot dogs and, damn it all, I think Twisties should be a food group.'

Leo shook his head. 'You don't mean that,' he said.

Sadie nodded. 'I'll tell you a secret about that girl, Leo. She wasn't happy. Not really. She just thought she was.'

Sadie couldn't look at the painting a moment longer. All she could see now was how starved for affection she'd been.

And she just wasn't that girl any more.

She turned on her heel and left. Left Leo standing in the middle of his studio gawping like a landed fish.

She took the stairs two at a time to her room and threw her things in her bag. As she headed out again she noticed a sketch pad and a box of sketching pastels on the bedside table. She fingered them lovingly—Leo was a creature of habit. He'd always kept stashes of them everywhere so he'd have access when the muse struck.

No doubt they were here because he'd thought they'd end up in bed together.

On a whim she picked them up and shoved them in her bag. Then she turned straight back around. She reached the front door just as Kent was entering. He looked so good, so *he-man*, so not *arty*, she almost threw herself straight at him.

But the wariness in his gaze as he took in her bag stopped her. 'We're leaving,' she said.

Kent blinked. They were supposed to stay another night with Sadie getting a plane to Darwin in the morning. He wasn't sure what had gone on in his absence but Sadie sounded pretty serious.

Hot but serious. That damn mouth he'd been thinking about all night set in a determined little line.

Just as the line of buttons down her front was taunting him.

'Give me five.'

She nodded. 'I'll wait for you in the car.'

Kent didn't ask any questions about Leo when he joined her in the promised five minutes. He just started the car. 'Where to?' he asked.

'Town,' she said. 'I need Twisties.'

Kent kept the food coming at a café in Borroloola and Sadie ate as if she were pregnant with twin elephants.

'Better?' he asked as she finally pushed away her plate and refused some more of his hot chips. It had given him immense satisfaction watching her load food into her mouth.

The painting of her in Leo's studio had been disturbing and he'd spent a lot of time out in the bush last night trying to scrub it from his brain. Understanding that the misogynistic idiot residing in Casa Del Leone was behind all her insecurities hadn't helped—seeing her eat did.

It also distracted him from the buttons.

And the kiss.

She nodded. 'I think I'm going to vomit, though,' she said as she rubbed her painfully full belly.

'Then my job here is done,' Kent mused as he sucked on his thick shake straw. She looked as if she'd been sprung from prison—or at least the chains from her past—and he was glad he was here to witness her first moments of freedom.

Sadie laughed, then groaned. 'Don't make me laugh or I really will throw up.'

Kent shrugged. 'You have tablets for that.'

'They're for motion sickness. Not gluttony.'

He laughed then and Sadie was relieved to see the wariness that had been in his gaze when they'd met at Leo's front door and on the silent trip into town seemed to have dissipated.

'What now?' he asked. 'Your flight doesn't leave until the morning. I can drop you at a hotel on my way out of town?'

Sadie shook her head. She didn't want to stick around any longer than she had to. 'You leaving for Darwin straight away?'

Kent nodded. 'It's about fifteen hours without stops for photos and a kip here and there.'

Sadie thought about it for a minute. Another night under the stars. With Kent.

Who had kissed her.

It didn't sound wise.

'Can I hitch a ride with you?'

Kent's gaze dropped to Sadie's mouth as the illicit request undulated towards him. He sobered as he dragged his eyes upwards. 'I didn't think you were keen to drive any further than you had to?'

Sadie nodded, noting the return of his wariness. And the way he'd looked at her mouth. Her heart started to beat a little faster. 'By the time my flight gets into Darwin tomorrow you'll already be there, right?'

'Probably,' he conceded.

'So it kind of makes sense to go with you.'

He nodded. 'It does.'

Which didn't stop him from knowing that being in a car with her for hours on end was not at all sensible. Nor was lying on a rooftop with her under the stars.

Not after the kiss.

'Please,' she asked quietly as his face remained in an uncompromising mask. 'I really just need to get as far away from Leo as possible.'

Well, now that reasoning he couldn't fault. If he had his way, he'd be on the other side of the planet to the man.

Sadie watched his features soften a little and quickly jumped in. 'I promise I'll be quiet as a mouse.'

Kent snorted as he pulled his wallet out and threw money on the table. 'I'll believe that when I see it Sadie Bliss.'

Sadie's vow of silence didn't last long in the car. 'About last night.'

Kent's grip tightened on the steering wheel. He flicked a glance at the dashboard clock. 'Ten minutes, Sadie, you're slipping.'

Sadie ignored him. She could feel the tension rolling off him and didn't want to spend fifteen hours absorbing the fallout. 'I think we need to talk about it… It's kind of the elephant in the car at the moment, don't you think?'

Kent shrugged. 'It happened. It shouldn't have. Let's leave it at that.'

Sadie blinked at the very neat summation of what had been going through her head. How surprising that Kent should be so succinct!

'It was just a kiss,' he dismissed as Sadie's silence worried him. 'It was a weird moment in a strange night.'

She nodded. It certainly had been. But it hadn't just been any old kiss. There'd been nothing friendly or brotherly about it. Nothing comforting. It might have been brief but for those few seconds she'd never felt so out of her depth.

'Stop it,' Kent said as the silence stretched loudly between them.

Sadie frowned. 'Stop what?'

'Stop humming the "Wedding March" in your head.'

Sadie glanced at him, alarmed. 'Don't flatter yourself,

Kent Nelson. It wasn't that good,' she lied. 'I'm not into strong silent times. I like to be able to converse with a potential future husband, not have to bargain for every word that comes out of his mouth.'

'Good.' He nodded, satisfied.

She glared at him, feeling tenser than when she'd first opened her mouth. 'There, now, don't you feel better it's all out in the open?' she asked sarcastically.

Kent didn't deign to answer and not least of all because the answer was no. All she'd done was put the kiss front and centre when he had been almost successful in burying it with the other stuff in his *do-something-about-it-later* box.

Sadie spent the next few hours feigning interest in the scrubby red-earth scenery but her brain was busy with other things. She couldn't work out whether she was more upset that he'd dismissed the kiss as nothing or that he'd kissed her in the first place. She certainly had relived it more times than was helpful when the man responsible for it and all its cataclysmic glory was just an arm's length away, those lips of his tantalising her peripheral vision.

Lips that knew how to get down to business.

By the time the dash clock hit five she desperately needed a distraction from the direction of her thoughts.

She glanced at Kent, his strong silent profile unchanged, an ear bud jammed in the ear closest to her. She reached over and pulled it out.

'Why haven't you done an interview since the accident?' she asked, her idea of a feature story on him returning.

Kent ignored her, not taking his eyes off the road. And to think her silence had lulled him into a false sense of security.

Sadie rolled her eyes. 'So we're back to ignoring me again?'

'If I thought it'd make a difference I just might.'

'You must have had offers,' she pressed when it became obvious he wasn't about to say anything else. 'It's a fascinating story.'

'Yes I have,' he said, gaze fixed on the white lines running up the centre of the highway.

'And?' Sadie prompted.

Kent turned his head and looked her straight in the eye. 'It's no one's damn business, Sadie.' He looked back at the road. 'What happened to me is private—very private. It's not for general consumption.'

Sadie got the message loud and clear. But it was pretty obvious Kent needed to talk to someone.

'What if I interviewed you? I'm pretty sure Leo's on the phone right now to Tabitha revoking all rights to the interview material so I'm going to need a back-up plan.'

'You have the road-trip story,' he dismissed.

'She wants two for the price of one, remember, and getting sacked on my first job is not good on the CV. I can't let her down. I need to deliver.'

Kent nodded. 'That's true. Tabitha doesn't like to be let down.'

Sadie gave an internal groan. *Excellent.* 'Is that a yes?'

Kent wrapped his fingers more firmly around the steering wheel. 'My story is not for sale.'

Sadie heard the same ice in his voice he'd used for telling her he didn't fly. Regardless, she prepared to launch into a whole selling patter because the thought of letting Tabitha Fox down was not a nice one, but mostly because she knew it'd annoy him.

And at least when he was angry at her she wasn't thinking about kissing him so much.

But an awful clunk coming from the general direction of the engine put paid to any further chit-chat.

'What was that?' she asked, clutching the door handle.

Kent slowed the still-running vehicle slightly as he looked at his instruments. 'I'm not sure,' he said after a moment or two. 'The temperature gauge is climbing, though.'

His eyes sought the road ahead, looking for the best place to pull over.

Fifteen minutes later Kent had parked the Land Rover under some large gum trees on the relatively flat stretch of highway. The other side of the road was less hospitable with a large expanse of scrub stretching almost uninterrupted to the horizon.

'What's wrong with it?' Sadie asked as she joined Kent beneath the bonnet.

'I think I've blown the water pump.'

Sadie looked at the convoluted metallic pipes of the internal combustion engine. It might as well have been an alien spacecraft. 'That sounds bad.' She looked at him. 'Is that bad?'

'It'll need a new one and if we were in Sydney I could probably find a dozen mechanics within two city blocks that had one in stock. Maybe not so much out here.'

Sadie chewed on her lip. 'Oh.'

Despite the fact that his hands were covered in grease, all Kent could smell was that damn passionfruit aroma of hers. Combined with her fate-worse-than-death look it was just plain irritating.

'It's okay, Sadie Bliss,' he said as he pulled the bonnet down and wiped his hands on an oily rag. 'You're not destined to be stuck in the outback for ever. I'm sure there'll be a garage in Borroloola that will be able to help.'

He left her by the front of the car and grabbed the satellite phone from the front seat. In ten minutes he'd located a supplier in Katherine who would send a tow truck by nine tomorrow morning. He hung up the phone. 'Better get comfortable. We're here for the night.'

Sadie looked at him, alarmed. 'We are?' She looked around her wondering how many spiders chose to call this speck on the earth home.

He nodded. 'It's okay, I have camp gear in the back. I'll build a fire for now and we'll sleep up top like we did the other night.'

'Right,' Sadie said faintly.

Except they hadn't kissed the other night...

Kent set her up in a fold-out chair beneath the shade of a tree with her fully charged laptop and then came and went unloading stuff from the back of his vehicle and gathering firewood. In an hour he was lighting the fire. Sadie half expected him to drop a couple of rabbits at her feet and then set about skinning them.

'How's it going?' he asked, nodding at the laptop. 'Did you get everything you wanted for Pinto's feature?'

Sadie blinked, momentarily confused by the question because she hadn't been tapping away about Leo at all. Instead she'd been writing about him. About the strong, silent, tough-guy enigma that both baffled and intrigued her.

'Oh, yes, good, thanks,' she lied, shutting the lid. 'Plenty of info.' The earthy aroma of wood smoke spiralled out to meet her as the first plume hit the air. 'What about you? Are you happy with the pics you got on your little expedition last night?'

Kent nodded as he knelt by the fire, slowly feeding it. 'Yep.'

'Can I see them?' she asked.

Kent looked up at her, surprised. 'Sure. My camera bag's in the car.'

Sadie retrieved it and Kent showed her how to scroll back to the pictures he'd taken the night before. It seemed more complicated than something off the space shuttle, but eventually she got the hang of it.

'What did we do before digital cameras with delete buttons?' she murmured as she viewed the images of the starry night and giant phallic termite mounds rising out of long grass and silhouetted in the moonlight.

'I wish I could see these bigger,' Sadie said, frustrated by the vast outback night condensed to one tiny image.

'USB lead in the camera bag—attach it to your laptop,' Kent said as he threw bigger logs onto the fire.

Delighted, Sadie hooked up his camera to her laptop and scrolled through the images again. She skimmed right through the ones of Leo and his monolith, slowing down as she got to Kent's outback shots.

'These are amazing,' Sadie breathed in awe. 'They're going to look spectacular in the feature.'

Kent nodded, more than a little pleased with the shots himself.

'How did it feel? Out there, taking them?' she asked.

Kent paused, surprised at her question. Surprised even more that he wanted to answer it. 'It felt…good.' As if the part of him that had died, or had at least been severely injured, was finally recovering. 'Familiar.'

Sadie realised she probably wasn't going to get any more from Mr Silent and contented herself going through the shots a second time, picturing them laid out in the magazine. When she was done she realised the shadows had grown quite long and evening was just about to fall around them. She shivered as the temperature suddenly seemed to plummet.

'Here,' Kent said, coming up behind her and plonking something around her shoulders.

Sadie hunched into the warmth of the fleecy flannelette shirt, like one of those cowboys always wore.

How fitting that Kent should own one.

'How does two-minute noodles and flambéed marshmallows sound?' he asked as he sat on the groundsheet he'd laid down earlier.

Sadie laughed. 'Will we be singing "Kum-ba-yah" too?'

Kent grunted as he set the billy in the fire to boil the water for the noodles. 'I don't sing.'

Sadie rolled her eyes. 'Don't sing. Don't fly. Don't talk. What do you do for fun, Kent Nelson?' she teased.

Kent looked up at her encased in his shirt. Long shadows formed on her cheeks from her eyelashes as the firelight played over her face and the sky behind her slowly faded to a deep purple. He tried not to think about the many fun things they could be doing right now.

Sadie held her breath for a second or two as the copper highlights flickered to life in Kent's gaze. And she didn't think it was from the fire.

'I flambé marshmallows,' he said.

He turned back to the billy and Sadie breathed again, the moment passing.

She asked him some technical questions to do with his photography, which got them through the noodles, but when she confessed to never having roasted marshmallows in a fire and she sat down beside him for tuition, things moved back to that state of awareness again and she knew he was feeling it too.

Kent laughed as he watched Sadie attempting to cook her marshmallow in the coals of the fire, too frightened to shove it right in and turn it into a little ball of flame.

He couldn't believe anyone could get to their twenties and not have done something so simple and so damn good.

'You're doing it wrong.' He tutted as she pulled off a lukewarm marshmallow and popped it into a mouth already moist and sticky.

Not something that was good for his sanity.

Her cheeks were flushed by the heat radiating from the fire and she looked like a teenager.

'They're supposed to be like this,' he said, pulling his out from the fire glowing brightly in the night like a meteor burning up on entry. He blew on it gently, putting it out, then pulled it off the end of his stick and dropped it into his mouth.

Sadie watched the process, fascinated. Who'd have thought lips that would have been perfectly at home on a statue would also look just as good coated in gooey marshmallow? Last night it hadn't even occurred to her to analyse how he tasted. It had been too quick, too intense. Now she couldn't think about anything else.

'Doesn't it taste burnt?' she asked, looking away as she realised she was staring.

He shook his head as he skewered another soft treat and held it above the coals. 'It tastes crunchy and then explodes in your mouth all hot and gooey.'

Sadie's mouth watered. And she was pretty sure it had nothing to do with the marshmallows.

Kent's marshmallow caught and he pulled it away, pushing the glowing orb her way. 'Here, just try it.'

Sadie shook her head. 'Won't it burn my fingers?'

Kent rolled his eyes as he blew on it and pulled it off. 'You're such a city girl.' He offered it to her quickly. 'Open up.'

Sadie shouldn't have opened up. But his fingers were

pushing it towards her lips and his tiger eyes were daring her and the treat smelled hot and sweet and sticky.

So she opened up.

Big mistake. The crunch melted against her tongue and soft sweet goo spilled into her mouth. Her senses filled with sugar and him. Flames danced shadows over his stubbly cheeks as she sucked every sticky morsel from his sweet warm fingertips. She saw his pupils dilate in the firelight.

Kent froze as his fingers lingered on her mouth completely of their own accord. His gaze lingered too. How could it not when her mouth glistened all sweet and sticky? Beckoned, even, and he was suddenly wondering what her marshmallow mouth tasted like.

'Oh, hell,' he muttered as he dropped his head to find out.

CHAPTER EIGHT

Sadie met him halfway, her heartbeat slow and thick as if marshmallow were running through her veins. His perfect mouth touched hers and there was nothing sweet and warm about it. It was hot and heady. Exploding inside her like a shower of sparks from the fire.

Heat shot to all her extremities. Lighting spot fires wherever it touched.

And she didn't care that they were in the middle of the bush or that they'd known each other for only a handful of days or that creatures lurked beyond the radius of the firelight.

She only cared about his hands in her hair, the brush of his thumbs at her temples, the heat of his mouth.

The harsh suck of his breath. The sweetness of lips. The deep rumble of his moan as her tongue found his.

And the driving imperative for more.

Her hands crept to his chest, bunched in his T-shirt, pulled him closer. She opened her mouth wider. Angled her neck back further. Kissed him harder.

Kent could feel Sadie trembling against him as their kiss raged out of control. Could feel the answering tremble in his gut. Every breath he took filled his head with her and lust beat like a jungle drum in his head, pounded through his veins, pulsed through his impossibly hard erection.

It was heady and addictive and he wanted more. He wanted her naked. Under him. Crying out his name.

All night.

And the one after that. And the one after that.

It was way too much, way too soon.

He tore his mouth away, his forehead pressed against hers, his breathing harsh in the vast outback evening.

Sadie mewed as her scrambled brain grappled with the abrupt disconnect. 'What?' she asked, her voice husky as she pulled back slightly, her hands dropping from his chest, her gaze locking with his.

Kent cleared his throat. 'This is…kind of out of control. It's heading pretty quickly in a direction you might not want it to go.'

Sadie frowned. 'I'm not sixteen, Kent. I know where this is heading.'

Kent swallowed as her gaze zeroed in on his mouth and the urge to kiss her again intensified. 'I can't offer you a relationship, Sadie.'

Sadie blinked. *Where in hell had that come from?* 'Just as well I only want to use you for sex, then.'

'Sadie,' he growled as his still rock-hard erection twitched.

Sadie ran her tongue over her lips, trying to savour the taste of him while he was being all adult. 'I'm not hearing the "Wedding March" if that's what you're worried about.'

Kent followed her tongue as it took a tour of her mouth. 'Don't do that,' he rasped as the action went straight to his groin.

Sadie heard the strain in his voice and smiled. 'What—this?' she asked, cocking an eyebrow as she sent her tongue around for a second swipe.

Kent felt every cell in his body tense. 'Sadie,' he warned.

'Or this?' she asked innocently as she reached for the packet of marshmallows, plucked one out and slipped it into her mouth.

'Mmm,' she murmured, shutting her eyes as she chewed, then deliberately pushed her hands into her hair, lifting it off the back of her neck before dropping it again and opening her eyes.

Sadie watched Kent's Adam's apple bob in his throat. She reached for another marshmallow, bringing it slowly to her mouth, touching it lightly to her lips before withdrawing it.

'You look like you could do with one of these,' she murmured, advancing it towards him, brushing it against his mouth.

Kent's lips tingled at the illicit gesture; he wasn't fooled by the innocence in her eyes or the soft baby pink of the offering.

It might as well have been shiny red because both of them knew it was an invitation to sin.

Their gazes locked as he opened his mouth and she gently pushed it in. 'Now this is my kind of fun,' she murmured.

She kept two fingers against his mouth as he slowly devoured it, admiring the way the fire illuminated the shadows of his face. When he was done he sucked her fingers into his mouth and removed the powdery marshmallow coating.

Then he hauled her into his lap and slammed his mouth against hers.

Sadie wasn't sure if she moaned or he did as sugar turned to spice but she gripped the front of his T-shirt as passion flared and their kisses became deeper, wetter, longer.

Desire squirmed in her belly, heated her thighs, tingled between her legs where the denim of his jeans rasped against her. She could feel the thud of his heart beating at one with hers.

The smell of wood smoke and man filled up her senses and their passion took on a primal quality. She rubbed herself against him. She wanted to strip off all her clothes and be naked with him, like the first man and woman.

As if they were the only two people on earth.

For one crazy moment out here in the middle of nature she even wished that this were her first time.

Kent was only vaguely aware of the cool air hitting his back as Sadie hauled his T-shirt up. Their contact was temporarily broken as he ducked out of it and he took the opportunity as he claimed her mouth again to shift, to tumble her onto the groundsheet, her hair spilling out around her head.

He propped himself on his side, his mouth leaving hers to explore lower, his hand coming to rest on her belly. He traced his tongue down her throat, dipping into the hollow at the base. She moaned and shifted restlessly, her body undulating in his peripheral vision, pushing her breasts up. His hand scrunched into the fabric of her dress as lust seared his groin with a fiery arrow.

He traced his tongue to her collarbone. Followed the path of her shoestring strap. Licked along the edge of her bodice. Dipped into the hint of cleavage.

She shifted again and her little whimper had him pulling back. He gazed down at her. Her eyes were closed, her beautiful full mouth parted. When her eyelids fluttered open her large grey eyes were cloudy with passion.

'I want to look at you,' he said as his hand drifted up over her breasts.

Sadie gasped, her eyelids flickering to half-mast as his fingers brushed an erect nipple.

Kent stopped his upward trajectory and brushed his thumb over the hard little bead he could feel scraping against his finger pad. 'You like that?' he murmured as Sadie gasped again and arched her back. He didn't give her a chance to reply as he dipped his head and put his mouth to the fabric, sucking hard.

Sadie hissed out a breath as she felt the pressure of Kent's tongue and the moistness of his mouth deep down in her centre. Her breasts had always been extraordinarily sensitive and she gripped his shoulder as he took his own sweet time with it. Her belly stirred and she shifted against the ground, each swipe of his tongue involuntarily arching her back. Her brain was utter mush when he finally lifted his head and turned his attention to her cleavage.

'These damn buttons have been taunting me all day,' he muttered as he popped the first one, then the next, then the next. His one-handed dexterity wasn't the best but he enjoyed the slow reveal of her pink bra with a familiar twinkling diamanté in the V of the cleavage.

Sadie's breath was ragged as she watched Kent patiently undo each button on her dress. *All forty of them.* He didn't appear to be in a hurry and when he finally parted the dress and it slithered off her body to pool at her sides he took his time, running his gaze over every centimetre of bare skin.

Sadie actually blushed.

She wasn't used to men taking their time or inspecting her so thoroughly.

'Kent.' She wasn't sure if it came out as eager or desperate but her whole body was humming with desire.

He dragged his gaze away from her body and looked down into her firelit face. 'You're beautiful, Sadie Bliss.'

Sadie's breath caught in her throat. 'You look pretty damn fine yourself,' she murmured.

Kent chuckled as he looked back down at two very magnificent breasts. Breasts he'd thought about a lot the last five days. He traced a finger up a creamy slope to the diamanté at the centre, then back down again. Goosebumps broke out on her skin and he looked at her. 'Cold?'

Sadie shook her head. 'I think I'm so hot I'm about to self-combust.'

He reached into the V and flicked open the front clasp, her large breasts spilling free. 'You can say that again,' he breathed reverently.

Sadie blushed at his scrutiny and tried to cover herself up out of habit. She'd spent a lot of years trying to disguise her breasts. For her father who'd wanted her to be a boy. For Leo who'd wanted them to be smaller. For her career so she could be taken seriously.

Kent pulled her arm away, planting it above her head as he stared at the perfection before him. 'Don't.'

She looked away from the wonder in his eyes, her belly squirming at his utter fascination. She'd seen that look too often when she'd got to this stage with previous partners. But in her experience they held more novelty value for men than forming any actual part of their sexual repertoire.

'They're too big,' she muttered as she stared into the fire, embarrassed.

'They're perfect.'

Sadie looked at him. 'Aren't you going to ask me if they're real?'

Kent shook his head as he cupped her breast where it naturally fell sideways. 'Nope. These,' he said, stroking his fingers along the generous side swell, 'are the real deal.'

And then, because he was practically salivating, he dropped his head and sucked a large round nipple deep into his mouth.

Sadie shut her eyes on a whimper that was almost primordial. His mouth was hot and her nipple even more so but it ruched as quickly as if Kent had placed an ice cube on it. She arched her back and he took it deeper.

Spots formed behind her eyes as he flicked his tongue and grazed his teeth across the sensitive nub. She cried out when he released it, from relief or frustration she wasn't sure, but it was short-lived as he bent to suckle the other, his fingers moving to continue the torturous possession of the one recently released.

Heat started to ripple in little pools deep inside her belly and she lifted her hips restlessly as she cried out, 'Kent.'

Kent lifted his head, desire pounding thick and sludgy through his veins. She looked utterly sexy with her head tossed back, her mouth parted and he quickly claimed it, plundering the soft recesses, soothing her whimpers with his tongue even as he stoked them higher by fondling and kneading her breasts.

'Oh, God,' Sadie whispered as Kent once again abandoned her mouth in favour of a nipple. She sucked in a breath, arching her back as his warm mouth closed over her and his fingers created havoc with the other.

Sadie couldn't think. She could barely breathe as she rode the intense sensations battering her body. The ripples spread further to her thighs and radiated to her buttocks as the world became just Kent—his bare broad shoulders and his hot, hot mouth.

She was sure she was drooling.

She was definitely very, very ready.

Kent pulled away to look at the moist peak he'd just been savouring glisten in the firelight. 'God, Sadie,' he groaned. 'I could do this all night.'

Sadie had a brief moment of clarity when she knew she'd never survive a night of this before he lowered his head to the closest nipple and the world went hazy again.

She cried out as his teeth grazed the tip, her muscles inside contracting hard at the sheer eroticism. Heat flooded into her pelvis. Her thighs grew heavy. Her belly tensed. She was barely aware of his hand finally relinquishing its torture of the other nipple as the ripples grew stronger, more rhythmic, syncing in with the swipes of Kent's tongue.

Kent's head spun at the desperate keening cries coming from somewhere at the back of Sadie's throat. Her arousal was heady and his erection throbbed at every appreciative little whimper. Her nipples were hard and tight against his tongue, a stark contrast to the warm gooey marshmallow from before but no less sweet.

His hand stroked down her abdomen, swirling around her belly button, brushing lower, her soft sighs playing like a cheer squad in his head.

His fingers brushed the edge of her underwear, soft and gauzy, the little diamanté that had taunted him that night in the bathroom hard as the nipple in his mouth. He moved lower still, tracing his fingertips down over the outside of the fabric, the weave of the filmy material imprinting on his fingerprints.

He followed the heat down, down, down as his tongue rolled over and over the peak of her taut nipple, his teeth grazing lightly with each pass. His finger dipped into the seam that parted her, whispering against the little nub engorged with sex, heat and lust.

Sadie bucked. One second his mouth was creating delicious havoc and the next, with just one brush of his finger, her world came apart. Release hit at warp speed, coalescing into a ball of heat and light and pressure right at her very core. The ripples became a tsunami and exploded through her internal muscles in spasms of almost unbearable pleasure.

She cried out his name into the night as her climax not

only shook her, but felt as if it shook the very foundations beneath her. The stars above her head twisted into pretty kaleidoscope patterns just before her lids shut them out and she gripped his shoulders to keep her earthbound.

It took a moment for Kent's lust-drunk brain to realise what was happening. His hand stilled and he lifted his head as he looked down into her firelit face as she gasped, her eyes shut tight, her head rocking from side to side.

Watching Sadie Bliss shatter into a million pieces was the sexiest thing he'd ever seen.

He'd never been so turned on in his life.

He'd lost his virginity at nineteen and he'd prided himself on always leaving a woman satisfied, but never in all the years since had a woman been *this* responsive.

He watched every last nuance of her climax as it rippled through her face from her scrunched brow to her parted mouth. He held her as her cries settled, her face relaxed and her eyes slowly opened, coming into a slow dazed-looking focus on his.

He smiled down at her. 'Why, Sadie Bliss, that's one hell of a party trick,' he murmured.

Sadie's brain scrambled to come back on line as her cheeks warmed. She saw amusement flickering in his gaze and shut her eyes again. She wanted to die. She wanted the earth to open up and swallow her. The man had barely touched her and she'd shattered into a thousand pieces like some seedy porn queen.

The exact behaviour every guy she'd ever been with had expected from a woman with a body like hers.

'I'm sorry,' she said, opening her eyes, pushing against his arms, desperately trying to pull the edges of her clothing together, suddenly ashamed of her nudity.

Kent frowned as she struggled to sit up. 'Sadie,' he said, firming his arms around her a little.

Sadie shook her head, panic setting in. She needed to get up, to cover up. To have a shower. To curl up in her bed and stick her head under the pillow. 'Let me up,' she demanded, pushing against him again.

Kent heard the note of alarm in her voice and instantly rolled back. 'Sadie, it's fine,' he said as she vaulted upright, scrambling to her feet, grasping at the edges of her clothes, keeping her back to him.

Sadie shook her head, her legs barely supporting her as her useless trembling fingers tried to button the dress. 'I'm sorry,' she said, battling with the insane urge to cry as the buttons refused to cooperate. 'I'm…they're very… sensitive and it's been a while.'

Sadie cringed even as she said it. What possible excuse was there to come in two seconds with someone who was practically a stranger? God knew what he thought of her.

Kent frowned. He couldn't for the life of him work out what was so awful about the situation. 'Why are you apologising?'

Sadie shut her eyes as the buttons defeated her. Keeping her back to him, she quickly shrugged out of his shirt, her dress and bra and then climbed back into the fleecy warmth of flannelette.

Kent, still hard, twitched at the glimpse of her bare thonged buttocks, another diamanté winking in the firelight where the back waistband was intersected by a thin vertical strip connecting the front with the back.

'Can we please just forget this happened?' she muttered, pulling the shirt edges together firmly across her chest, knowing buttons were still beyond her.

She really didn't want to talk about this.

Kent watched as his shirt enveloped the backs of her thighs and the view was snatched away.

'Look at me, Sadie.'

Sadie hugged her waist and contemplated melting into the dark outback night. Anything seemed preferable to facing him after her completely wanton behaviour.

Even the spiders and scorpions seemed a reasonable risk.

How many could there be?

But, there were times for putting on her big girl pants and this was one of them. She hugged her waist harder as she turned to face him. 'I'm sorry,' she said again, looking at the ground.

Kent stood but stayed where he was. Sadie looked as if she was going to bolt off into the bush at any moment and he didn't want to scare her. 'You should never apologise for enjoying sex, Sadie. Never.'

He cringed as soon as he said it. He sounded just like his high-school sex-ed teacher and the last thing he needed to do now with Sadie looking utterly mortified was to come across as if he were the mature voice of reason and she were a child.

Especially considering what had happened was very, very adult!

Sadie looked at him incredulously. 'We didn't even get to the sex bit.'

He didn't understand. How could he? She felt as if she needed to clarify. To put the experience in context.

'I'm sorry,' she apologised again, returning her gaze to the ground because the firelight on his chest was doing funny things to nerves still hypersensitive to stimuli. The low crackle of the campfire and the trill of insects were the only witness to her discomfort.

'I know I probably just came across as inexperienced but it's not that... Men don't ever usually...not really anyway, you know...take the time with...to...you know... with...them...' she tightened her arms across her chest and cleared her throat '...and you did. So, sorry I...you know...got there...a little...early.'

Kent frowned. Was she saying what he thought she was saying? 'I don't understand? Are you saying that the men you've been with haven't appreciated your...assets?'

Sadie blushed at the incredulity on his face. She suddenly preferred it when they weren't talking. But given what had just happened, they couldn't pretend they were just travelling companions any more.

And she really needed him to understand her rather over-the-top reaction to a bit of heavy petting.

She tossed her hair. 'Oh, they appreciate them well enough. Like a status symbol, you know? Check out my phone. My car. My girlfriend's knockers. But when it gets down to...the business...they usually get pretty neglected.'

Kent frowned again. 'Are men on the dating scene intellectually impaired these days?' He could have spent all night fondling her breasts.

Especially when she was so goddamn appreciative!

Hell, he could get off on her getting off alone.

Sadie shook her head, ashamed at the words that were forming there. At the horrible truth of them. About what they said about her more than an indictment on the men she'd been with.

Of what she'd put up with.

'Men form an impression of me...of what I'd be like in the sack...because of my bra size. They want pneumatic Barbie but sex is usually more about them than me.' Certainly it had been for Leo, but love had blinded her to that until tonight. 'I sometimes feel like I'm starring in some kind of wham-bam-thank-you-ma'am porn movie where it's all about looking the part and the end result rather than the journey.'

Kent looked at her, horrified. 'So you just let them?'

Sadie shook her head, frustrated as she transferred her gaze to the fire, trying to think of a way to explain it. 'Don't get me wrong. I enjoy sex, I like…the end result. It's not bad…it's just not…' She didn't know how to explain it other than the truth, which she hadn't realised until tonight with Kent.

She looked at him standing in nothing but his jeans, the warm yellow light shading the fascinating musculature of his abdomen in interesting shadows.

'Like tonight. Like the journey mattered more.' She held his gaze. 'I'm sorry it just…happened.'

Kent shook his head. 'Don't be sorry. I've never been so turned on in my life.'

Sadie swallowed. His voice was deadly serious and her belly contracted. She saw the flare of heat in his eyes, which she didn't think had anything to do with the fire. She was acutely aware of their state of undress. Of what they'd been doing just a few minutes ago.

'Oh, God,' she said, clutching the two edges of the shirt tight at her cleavage as she realised that, whilst she might be pretty damn satisfied, he'd been left in the lurch. 'You must be…' she blushed. 'Do you want to…? I mean, I can help you with…'

She took a step towards him feeling like a virgin again as her gaze dropped to the area between where his hands bracketed his hips.

Was there a discernible bulge there?

Kent held up a hand. 'It's fine. I'm pretty sure I won't die from going without,' he said drily.

She took another step, appalled at leaving him hanging. And also feeling the heat starting to stir again as she wondered what he could possibly do with other parts of his anatomy if he could do what he'd done with his mouth. 'Oh, but—'

Kent stepped back, shaking his head. 'No, wait. I'd rather just…look at you. Can I?'

Sadie glanced at him warily. 'What do you mean?'

'I'd like to look at you,' he said throatily. 'At the fire-light on your skin.'

Sadie tightened her hold on the shirt. Night had well and truly fallen around them now and the glow of the campfire was the only light. The road was silent. It was just them and the stars.

Kent held out his hand, his heart pounding in his chest. Sadie had been hiding her body because a few lousy men didn't know how to treat a woman. He wanted to show her she had nothing to be ashamed of and there was one way he knew how to do that better than any other.

Sadie swallowed. He looked so serious, but her insides had turn to mush at his husky request and whilst he was looking at her as if she were the only woman in existence she'd probably do just about anything he wanted.

She took his hand and let him pull her down to the groundsheet until they were sitting cross-legged opposite each other, close but not touching.

'Do you mind?' he asked as he reached over for his camera bag.

Sadie felt everything deep down inside her squeeze. He wanted to photograph her?

Posing, she knew.

Posing, she could do.

But in this medium? With this man? Who'd known her for five days but had still managed to give her the most intense sexual experience of her life?

It was equal parts titillating and scary.

She nodded, not trusting her voice.

Kent dipped in and pulled the camera out. He looked through the lens at her face as he made some adjustments, knowing without a doubt as he studied her features that he had his mojo back.

Her eyes were cast downwards and her hair had fallen forward. She made no attempt to push it back, as if she was deliberately trying to hide.

Suddenly she looked right at him, her knuckles white as they gripped his shirt tight across her chest at the lapels. 'What do you want me to do?'

'Whatever you want,' he murmured as he snapped off the first shot.

He watched as she sat awkwardly beneath the eye of the all-seeing lens, snapping away. The fire glowed on one side of her face, throwing the other side into relief. He concentrated on the shadows, how they shaded her profile, her eyelashes, her cheekbones, the pout of her mouth, the jut of her chin.

Sadie tossed her head and looked right in the lens finally. A little frown knitted her brows together.

'You'll get wrinkles,' he murmured.

Sadie poked her tongue out at him and said, 'Hey,' when he captured it in a split second.

He chuckled and she smiled. Suddenly self-conscious, she scrunched her hair, fluffed it a bit. 'This is what I used to look like,' she said, forming a little moue with her mouth and sucking in her cheeks as Kent clicked.

Kent shuddered at the image from Leo's studio wall. 'You looked terrible.'

Sadie scrunched her face. 'Gee, thanks.'

Kent caught the scrunch with a quick press of a button. 'I mean it, Sadie, you looked like you had a terminal illness.'

Sadie looked at him through his camera, a little frown between her brows. She'd held Leo's images of her up in her mind for so many years as the idyll of feminine lure, had lived in its shadow, it was surprising to realise it wasn't actually true.

'So…the painting…' she hesitated '…didn't work for you?'

Kent dropped the camera to look at her. 'You want to know what works for me? Let your shirt go, Sadie. I'll show you.'

Sadie's breath stuttered to a halt in her throat for a few seconds. Things shifted deep inside her and she was suddenly incredibly nervous. Portraits took weeks, months. Film was instant. There was something about the immediacy of a camera, the up-close intrusion of the lens, that made her want to run for the hills.

She tossed her head. 'So you're not really any different from Leo, then? You also want me to strip off my clothes for your art?'

Kent could hear the quiver in her voice and see the resentment on her face. He hated the comparison to that misogynistic bastard, but he shook his head calmly. 'I want to look at you. See you. As you are. Not my *interpretation* of you. Just you. In all your amazing, curvy glory. I want to show you.'

Sadie could feel herself blushing beneath the intensity of his gaze, the copper flecks glowing in the firelight.

Could she just be her?

'You're beautiful, Sadie. Let me show you.'

Sadie swallowed. His request whispered to her on the still night air and oozed into all those places that had ever harboured doubts about her body. She could feel the chains of Leo's conditioning loosen.

Could Kent be right?

Was *this* Sadie Bliss, *the real one*, beautiful?

She looked down as she slowly let go of the shirt, her hand falling in her lap, the edges parting slightly. The chill had started to encroach as the fire dwindled and it stroked cool fingers over the hint of exposed cleavage.

Kent exhaled slowly as he caught a glimpse of creamy flesh. His erection made an instant resurgence but he didn't say a word, just put the camera back to his face and started snapping again. She didn't move for a while, her hair falling forward masking her face, and he didn't ask her to, just snapped away, being patient, waiting for her to make the first move.

Sadie glanced up at him through her hair, the constant click and whirr of the camera loud between them. She rolled her shoulders back a little, exposing more of her chest, her nipples beading despite still being covered. She looked at the lens more directly.

'I better not see any of these on the Internet,' she joked.

Kent smiled as he clicked. 'That's the beauty of the delete button.'

Sadie pushed her hair back behind her ear, the shirt lifted and opened some more.

'Lay back a little,' Kent murmured, his voice husky as his erection surged against the confines of his jeans.

Sadie felt his words go right to her pelvic floor. She waited a beat before complying. Placing her palms flat on the groundsheet behind her, automatically thrusting her chest outwards. She heard the snap, snap, snap and dared a little further, shaking her hair as she fell back onto her bent elbows.

'Like this?' she asked. The shirt gaped open covering only the tips of her breasts now.

Kent swallowed. 'Fabulous,' he croaked.

Sadie bent both her knees up and tipped her head back, shrugging her shoulders as she did so, rippling the shirt right off her breasts, fully exposing them. Her nipples were painfully tight from cold and the illicitness of their nature shoot.

'This okay?' she murmured, shutting her eyes as the warmth from the fire heated one side of her body.

Kent dropped the camera from his face momentarily. She looked as if she were moon-baking, her face raised to the heavens in silent supplication. 'Perfect,' he murmured, the camera forgotten as he drank in the creamy palate of skin bathed in a yellow glow.

Sadie lifted her head and looked at him, at the heat in his gaze. She felt suddenly liberated baring her all to him. Flaunting her body instead of trying to de-emphasise it.

Thankful more than he'd ever probably know that he'd rescued her from a mindset that had held her prisoner too long.

She parted her lips and gave him a Mona Lisa smile. Her heart beat a little faster as she let the leg closest to the fire flop to the side, the movement shifting deliciously through her torso. 'What about this?' Her underwear was laid bare to him and she watched as his gaze dropped to check it out.

Kent swallowed as she lay almost completely exposed to his view. The diamanté decorating her pink thong winked at him as his gaze fanned upwards, over the gentle rise of her belly, up to the swell of her breasts, the nipples standing hard and proud beneath his gaze.

She looked so damn perfect he wanted to eat things off her.

Twisties. He wanted to eat Twisties off her.

He ignored the direct order coming from his pants to cease and desist with the camera already and get down to business. Sadie was looking at him with power in her gaze, with pride, and he was determined to give her this moment. He picked up the camera and snapped away again, recording every delectable dip and curve.

'You should never hide any of this, Sadie. You're glorious. You should be proud of it. Embrace it.'

Sadie was officially turned on knowing he was watching her intently through the lens, his gravelly words soothing to an ego that had been battered and bruised for a long time. She shifted her still-bent leg until the foot was resting on his calf, then she slowly traced her big toe up to his knee and down his thigh before coming to rest on the bulge behind his zipper.

'What about this?' she asked, her voice husky as she idly traced her toe over the hard ridge.

Kent dropped the camera, shutting his eyes as he sucked in a breath at the erotic torture. He cracked open his eyes as he placed a stilling hand on her foot. 'Ever done it on the roof of a car?'

Sadie smiled as she pushed the ball of her foot against the hard length of him. 'I don't think those swags are conducive to fooling around in and it's getting pretty cold.'

Kent's erection surged against the pressure. 'Lucky for us they zip together.'

'Really?' Sadie smiled. She withdrew her foot and in one fluid movement got to her feet.

'That's a yes, then?' He smiled, enjoying the view as he looked up at her. His shirt had never looked so damn good. It was completely open, exposing both breasts and the jut of her hard nipples. That fascinating pink gauzy patch at eye level.

'Hurry,' she tossed over her shoulder as she headed towards the vehicle.

Kent watched her go, firelight at her back, starlight at her front. He picked up his camera. 'Sadie,' he called.

Sadie half turned and smiled at him as he snapped the

perfect silhouette. His shirt was half off her shoulders, the
starry night an amazing backdrop.

'I'm getting naked in ten seconds and it's cold over
here,' she said as she continued on her way.

Kent didn't need to be told twice.

CHAPTER NINE

KENT woke with a start in the middle of the night to a noise. The first thing he saw was Sadie's concerned face looking down at him. He knew without having to ask that the noise must have come from him.

'You okay?' she asked. She'd gone to sleep with her head resting on Kent's shoulder and his head thrashing had woken her a few seconds ago.

Kent raised his head, blinking a couple of times as he looked around, trying to clear the clinging debris of his recurrent bad dream.

He sometimes wondered if he'd ever be okay again.

'Sorry.' He grimaced, his head falling back down.

Sadie resumed her position, snuggling into his side, tucking her head into his shoulder. He smelled good—like wood smoke, soap and man. Her palm sat against his chest and she could feel the accelerated thump of his heart. She shivered as he traced his fingers up and down her bare arm.

She didn't say anything for a while, content after their exhaustive rooftop session to lay snuggled against him under the stars.

'You have bad dreams?'

Kent's caress stilled momentarily before starting again. 'Yes.'

Sadie wasn't fooled by the evenness of his tone. His

thudding heart told another story. 'You had one that first night, too,' she said. She waited for him to say something and when nothing was forthcoming she glanced at his profile. 'Is it about the accident?'

'Yes.'

Sadie gently rubbed her palm along the pillow of a sturdy pec. 'I'm guessing you don't talk about it much?'

'Nope.'

'Maybe you should talk to a professional?' she suggested gently.

'Nope.'

Sadie's hand stilled on his chest and she rolled up onto her side, propping her head in her hand. 'Oh, dear,' she mused, watching his mouth in the moonlight. 'Are we back to the beginning again?'

Kent dropped his hand from her shoulder and looked at her. 'I'm not telling some strange shrink my problems.'

Sadie heard a world of pain and denial behind his vehement rejection of help. 'So don't,' she said, finally giving into the urge to trace his mouth with her finger, pulling it away when he shook his head from side to side to displace it. 'Talk to me about it instead.'

And before he could say no to her face she dropped down beside him again, placing her head on his shoulder, his hand automatically coming to rest there again.

Kent looked up at the stars, conscious of Sadie's naked body draped all warm and pliant against his. Every breath he took was filled with a special mix of cool outback and her and immersed him in memories from their fun beneath the covers not that long ago.

There was something extraordinarily generous about Sadie Bliss. She was a giver. And that had obviously cost her in life. She'd been a very generous lover. Making him laugh, making him want, making him hope more than he had since the accident.

All he'd wanted for two years was to feel better and here on a rooftop in the middle of nowhere, under a canopy of stars, he doubted he'd *ever* felt better.

She had sat in front of his camera tonight and bared more than just her body to him. She'd been naked and vulnerable in the truest sense of the word.

Maybe he could reciprocate?

'I hear Dwayne Johnson crying out for his mother.'

The words fell into the cold night air, stark and tinged with anguish, dragging Sadie out of a drowse. It had been quiet for so long, Sadie had assumed he'd drifted off or just wasn't going to talk about it at all.

For a moment she wasn't even sure what she should do or say. But then her hand automatically smoothed along his chest from one nipple to the other and she said, 'That must be difficult.'

Kent was relieved when Sadie didn't try to go all amateur psychologist on him. A few days ago he wouldn't have even contemplated telling her, worried that an intrusive, chatty, stacked twenty-four-year-old would go all Freudian on him.

But he'd learned a lot about Sadie Bliss in the last couple of days. She was much more than an arachnophobic girly.

'It's not every night,' he said. 'But it's…disturbing when it happens.'

Sadie pressed a kiss to his shoulder without conscious thought. She couldn't even begin to imagine the trauma Kent had been through. 'Tell me about *Mortality*.'

Kent tensed. 'That bloody picture,' he murmured.

'You don't like it?'

Kent shook his head. 'You told me that when you saw

it, in New York, you couldn't look at it because it was too private.' He shrugged. 'That's the way I feel about it too.'

'So how'd it make the cover of *Time*?'

'A journo friend of mine handed the camera over to my editor when I was in emergency surgery. I lost some days immediately after the crash. They operated four times in thirty-six hours and it was all a bit of a fog. The pictures were the least of my worries. When I finally came to my senses they were all over the media.'

'Couldn't you have them withdrawn?'

He nodded. 'I tried, but Dwayne's parents asked me if I would reconsider. They wanted the world to know that their son had died defending his country.'

'Bit hard to say no to that,' Sadie mused.

Kent chuckled at her understatement, surprised that he could laugh amidst it all. He gave her shoulder a squeeze. 'Yes.'

Sadie lay there absorbing the information for a while. 'At the risk of annoying you...' she said tentatively, not wanting to kill the mood. Obviously Kent talking about this torrid time in his life was not an easy thing but something was bugging her. 'I know you think I talk too much and—'

'Just say it, Sadie,' Kent interrupted on a sigh as tension crept into his belly muscles.

Sadie could feel the cosy mood evaporating but she'd come too far to back out, and if she was the only person he ever spoke to about this then maybe it was up to her to ask the difficult question. The question that had crowded into her brain when she'd first laid eyes on the photograph in that swanky New York gallery.

'I don't understand...how you even...took the photos in the first place?' There was more silence from Kent so she pressed on. 'I mean you were injured, right? Trapped in the body of a crashed helicopter, pinned by your ankle? Men you'd been embedded with for two months were dead and dying.' She pushed herself up and looked down at him. 'How do you stay on task when there's chaos around you?'

Keeping his cool in a situation had never been an issue for Kent. He'd cut his teeth in war zones. It was hard for anyone who didn't live that kind of life to understand.

He didn't look at her as he answered.

'It's my job to snap pictures when all around me is going to hell.'

Sadie would have to have been deaf not to hear the defensive tone in his voice. 'I'm not judging you, Kent. I'm just…curious.'

Kent grappled with telling her politely to mind her own damn business and the strange urge to talk to her. She'd been about the only person he'd ever met who hadn't tried to blow smoke up his arse about *Mortality*. She'd told him how unsettling the image was and he had the feeling she might just understand.

'I didn't want to take the damn pictures,' he finally muttered, looking at her. 'I was trapped. I could smell jet fuel and smoke. I was pretty sure I was about to die in a fiery inferno or by a bullet in the head from the guys that had shot us down.'

Kent wasn't sure if it was the last remnants of the campfire, but he swore he could still smell the smoke. How many times had he woken with the acrid stench in his nostrils?

'My leg hurt like hell. The very last thing on my mind was to snap off some pictures.'

Sadie raised her hand and gently brushed it over his eyes, his cheeks, his mouth. 'But you did?'

Kent nodded, remembering that day in all its Technicolor horror. 'The pilot, Johnny Lieberman, he was also trapped up front. He asked me if I was taking pictures.'

Sadie remembered that the pilot had died a few days later in an ICU in Germany from the wounds inflicted by the crash.

'I said no. *No, I'm not taking bloody pictures.* I couldn't believe he was even asking. I wasn't even sure where my camera was at and frankly I didn't care.'

'But you found it?'

'Johnny was adamant that I should. In fact, he ordered me to do it. Not that he could but he did anyway. Said people should know about this part of war. That helicopters crashed, that good men died. That hearing about it on the news and seeing a burnt-out shell after everything was cleaned up was different from looking at pictures taken in the middle of hell.'

Sadie traced his lips with her finger. 'So you took them.'

He nodded. 'I couldn't see a lot from my vantage point. Wreckage and desert and sky.'

'And Dwayne Johnson.'

Kent nodded. 'He'd been thrown clear so I had a…' Kent shut his eyes as the young soldier's cries played through his mind again. 'A really clear shot of him. I could see the life ebbing from his eyes through the lens. He was calling for his mother. He was frightened and I didn't want him to die alone. I tried to get out, to free myself.'

Sadie could only imagine how frantic Kent must have felt. 'But you couldn't,' she whispered.

The stars above him suddenly blurred, developing auras as if it had been raining in heaven, and it took him a moment to realise the moisture was in *his* eyes. He blinked rapidly. 'All I could do was take pictures.'

Sadie looked down into his face. She could just make out a shimmer of moisture in their copper-brown recesses.

She kissed him lightly. What else could she do? How was someone supposed to go through such a trauma and come out the same person at the end? For some things there were no words—just comfort and consolation.

'I'm so, so sorry,' she murmured against his mouth. Kissing him again.

Kent kissed her back, pushing his hands into her hair as he pulled her head down onto his mouth hard and fast, all the anguish and pain and frustration he'd felt over the last two years injected into the moment. Her lips tasted sweet and he wanted to get lost in her, in her mouth, her body, her moans and her sighs.

To not think for one night about Dwayne Johnson and a photo that still haunted him.

To affirm life.

He shifted, rolled towards her, rolled her under him as she opened her mouth to him, opened her legs to him.

He plundered her mouth as his hands moved lower, feeling her buck as he skimmed a breast and stayed to rub his thumb over the rapidly ruching nipple.

'Condom,' she muttered as she wrapped her legs around his waist, felt the thick hard bulk of him butting against her.

Kent blindly reached for the box inside her backpack that she'd brought up with her earlier and was stashed near their heads.

Where the hell was it, damn it?

'Hurry,' Sadie muttered in his ear as the temptation to have him drive into her then and there beat like insect wings inside her brain. She was ready, he was ready and she wanted to take him away somewhere far removed from an Afghan desert.

Kent finally located the box, grabbed a foil packet out and quickly donned the protection. Sadie reached for him and he settled back into the cradle of her pelvis, kissing her long and hard as he pushed deep inside her.

She cried out, the sound primal in their own rooftop Eden. Her fingertips bit into the flesh of his shoulders as he ground into her, each thrust driving higher and harder, pushing her closer. His mouth left hers, seeking a nipple, sucking it into his mouth as he rocked into her.

Kent lifted his head and groaned as his building climax dug fiery fingers deep into his buttocks, his arms anchored either side of her trembling as they held him up.

'Yes, yes, yes,' Sadie whispered as she too felt the bubble rising inside her.

He buried his face in her neck as everything spiralled out of control. He tried to hold it back, to hold them in the moment where things hung on a precipice between pleasure and completion, but the primal call was too strong for him and he let the wave sweep him away as she tightened around him and joined him in the maelstrom.

Sadie woke again as the sky was just starting to lighten. The stars were still out but waning as obsidian faded to velvet. Kent was sleeping, the first violet hues of dawn lying gently against his number-two stubble and beautiful mouth. She wanted to wake him but, between an insatiable sex drive and an obviously exhausting dream, his night had been disturbed enough.

She felt around her for his shirt which had been discarded somewhere in the bedding, finally locating it down by her foot. God alone knew where her thong was. She had a feeling Kent might have tossed it over the side.

The air still felt cool and she dragged the shirt on, doing up three buttons as she sat up, the sky too resplendent to miss. She reached behind her into her bag, pulling out the sketch pad and pastels she'd taken from Leo's, inspired again as she had been the other night under the stars when she hadn't had access to materials.

She sat with her back to Kent facing the road and the uninterrupted view in that direction. All that could be heard as the morning lightened to soft baby blues was the scratching of the pastels on the paper as Sadie sketched like a woman possessed, hurrying to capture the moment that night faded and dawn encroached before it was lost to her for ever.

She was so utterly absorbed in the process she didn't even feel Kent stir until he was behind her, pressing a kiss into her neck, peering over her shoulder.

She shut her eyes as he rumbled, 'Good morning,' in her ear.

She sighed, snaking a hand behind her and anchoring it around his neck, her fingers stained with a multicoloured chalky residue. She settled against his broad naked chest as his arms encircled her waist.

She felt stiff from sitting hunched over the sketch pad and she stretched a little as she said, 'Morning.'

Kent looked down at the sketch pad, the drawing arresting him immediately. It had captured the essence of an outback dawn with the vivid colours and swirls around the fading stars similar to those used by Van Gogh in his famous starry night painting, and yet there was something uniquely contemporary Australian about it.

It was an incredible blend of old world charm and modern boldness. It was simply stunning.

'Sadie…' He shook his head. 'That's…amazing.'

Sadie blushed at the compliment. 'It's just a sketch,' she dismissed, used to disregarding her work.

Kent shook his head. 'No, it's not. It's…a work of art.'

Sadie gave a half-laugh. She liked what she saw, and creating it had felt incredible, but she could see its flaws and felt the old doubts return. Could hear Leo's *you're not talented enough* mantra in her head.

'I couldn't not,' she said absently, looking down at the sketch. 'When I woke up and saw the sky, I couldn't not capture it. I *had* to do it.'

Kent heard the surprise in her voice. 'Well, that says a lot, doesn't it?' he murmured.

Sadie frowned as she half turned to look at him. 'What does it say?'

'You're an artist, Sadie Bliss. And whatever the hell you're doing with this journalism gig is just wasting your time. You were obviously born to do this.'

Sadie shook her head as she turned back to the sketch. 'No. I'm not good enough.'

Kent tightened his hand around her belly. 'Says who? Leonard Pinto?'

Sadie shrugged. 'The man does have an eye for art.'

Kent felt irrationally angry that one man could screw with a woman's head so much. 'Leonard paints women who look like boys. I think his eye is seriously off. I also think he knows *exactly* how talented you are but he didn't want to let you go.'

Sadie wanted to deny it but hadn't she come to the same conclusion yesterday? That he'd wanted his muse back and he was prepared to go to any lengths to get it?

Kent gentled his hands against her and lightly circled his thumbs over the curves of her hips. 'Sadie, you are *incredibly* good. Don't you think you owe it to yourself to explore that a little more?'

Sadie shut her eyes as his words of praise, aided and abetted by the brush of his thumbs against her skin and the scrape of stubble at her neck, seduced her.

A fledgling ray of possibility sparked to life inside her and she shied from it. Art had made her incredibly happy.

And incredibly unhappy. Could she go back to that roller coaster again?

She pushed the illicit thought away, stamping on its lure. It wasn't something she could decide on a whim. Certainly not on a car rooftop with a man who had already muddled her senses a little too much.

'I think,' she said, injecting playfulness into her tone, 'you're just saying that to get in my pants, Kent Nelson.'

Kent smiled as he nibbled at the place where her neck met her shoulder. She was obviously changing the subject but he had to give her points for her method.

'Well, now, that'd be kind of hard considering I pitched them somewhere over the side last night.'

Sadie smiled, letting herself get lost in the sexiness of his voice, taking her away from the serious stuff for a while. 'Kent Nelson,' she murmured. 'Are you suggesting I'm not wearing any underwear?'

Kent chuckled as he trailed his hand from her hip downwards. 'Well, now, why don't I check?'

Sadie shut her eyes as he confirmed what they both knew very quickly.

'Mmm,' he murmured, his other hand travelling north as his tongue traced patterns on her neck. 'You feel good.'

Sadie bit her lip as his hand cupped a breast. She tried to turn but he tightened his arms around her.

'Shh,' he said. 'Lean back and enjoy.'

Not an offer she could refuse.

The tow truck arrived at nine as promised and before they knew it they were sitting in the front of a poorly sprung truck next to an ancient local who chatted away merrily. A local who was thankfully oblivious to the fact that Sadie's fingers kept brushing lightly against the firm bulge behind Kent's zipper. And the way Kent's fingers caressed the swell of her breast under the guise of a casual arm slung over her shoulder.

It was a long, sexy, three-hour journey back to Katherine.

When they got into town Sadie opted for a café to do some work on her laptop whilst Kent saw to the vehicle. But not before he'd dragged her into the deserted toilets at the garage, pushed her against the wall and kissed her senseless, promising retribution for the torture she'd put him through.

Which made it difficult to concentrate on the story for Tabitha. So instead she spent her time in the café madly journalling the last few days with Kent. Words, like the strokes of the pastels this morning, flowed freely and she wasn't sure how much time had passed when a pair of worn jeans came into her line of vision.

She looked up from her screen and Kent smiled at her.

'I called your name twice. The story's shaping up nicely, then?'

Sadie tried not to look guilty as she smiled back at him. 'I think Tabitha will be happy,' she lied. 'Is the Land Rover ready?'

He nodded. 'Have you eaten?'

'Three cappuccinos, a muffin and a burger with the lot.'

Kent laughed at the sparkle in her doe eyes. 'Good. I'll order something to go and then we can hit the track.'

They were heading north to Darwin fifteen minutes later.

'Let's play I Spy,' Sadie said as she opened the packet of Twisties Kent had purchased back at the café.

Kent rolled his head to look at her briefly before looking back at the road. 'You think because we bonked like bunnies last night that I'll do anything for a repeat performance?'

Sadie grinned as she bit down on the cheesy snack, flavour exploding in her mouth. 'Yep.'

He laughed. *She was right.* 'You think I'm that easy?'

Sadie shrugged, examining a fat orange finger of pure carbohydrate. She brushed it against her mouth and sucked it slowly in. 'I could make it worth your while.'

Kent's gaze snagged on the orange dust clinging to her mouth. 'We're not talking about hand feeding me Twisties here, are we?'

She smiled as she plucked another out of the bag and licked it before she popped it into her mouth. 'Nope.'

'You're talking trading sexual favours?'

'Yep.'

'I *love* your dirty mind.'

Sadie laughed. She *loved* how he looked at her—as if he'd already stripped her naked.

Leo had looked at her as if he could fix her.

Kent looked at her as if she was already perfect.

'I spy with my little eye, something beginning with…' she pulled another Twistie out of the packet and poked it into her cleavage '…T,' she said, looking up when she was satisfied with the placement.

Kent's breath hitched in his chest as saliva coated his mouth. He was reminded of how he'd thought about eating Twisties off her body last night and he was hard in under ten seconds. 'How about we play truth and dare instead?' he suggested, his voice rough and low.

'Truth and dare,' Sadie mused as she placed a second in her cleavage.

'I dare you to strip down to your underwear and stay that way until we get to Darwin.'

He held his breath as he waited for her reply. The Sadie from a couple of days ago would have flayed him alive at the suggestion. Hell, the Kent from a couple of days ago would never have suggested it. But this Sadie, hell-bent on decorating herself in snack food, looked as if she was up for something totally spontaneous.

He certainly was.

Sadie felt her breath thicken in her throat and her nipples bead at his indecent proposal. 'Sure. But I dare you not to touch. Think you could manage that?'

Kent's pulse wooshed through his ears. She looked so damn sure of herself and he was torn between being the dare-taking kid of old who'd do anything to win and knowing that, if she really did get down to her underwear, it would only be a matter of time before he folded.

He nodded. 'Absolutely.'

Sadie smiled at the bob of his throat. 'Okay, then.'

Kent tried really hard to concentrate on the road, but it was difficult with Sadie shimmying out of her clothes in his peripheral vision. In under a minute she was sitting in some hot-looking red and black matching underwear—Twisties protruding from her cleavage.

Sadie tossed her clothing on the floor and smiled at him. 'I give you—' she looked at the clock '—five minutes.'

Kent kept his eyes firmly trained on the road. 'Easy,' he scoffed.

'Yes.' She smiled as she shoved another lurid orange finger into her bra. 'I know.'

Kent tapped his foot as the minutes slowly ticked by and Sadie shoved more Twisties everywhere. Her hair, her bra straps, snuggled against her nipples, her belly button.

At four minutes and thirty seconds she pulled the band of her knickers out and dropped one down the front, closing it with a snap.

'Right!' Kent said, indicating abruptly as he took the car cross country, right off the road. 'You win.'

* * *

The three-hour trip took about double that by the time he'd relieved her of all the hidden food and licked all the Twistie dust off her and she'd eaten a few off him. It was early evening when they drove into the outskirts of Darwin.

Kent looked at Sadie as she stared out of the window. She'd been curiously quiet the last hour or so. 'Cat got your tongue, Sadie Bliss?'

Sadie turned and smiled at him. She'd been conscious of their time running out and it was making her wistful. 'I didn't think you liked me chattering?'

'Since when did that stop you?'

Sadie ignored him. Since their relationship, or whatever the hell it was now, had moved to another level, since they'd both got to know each other a little better, she didn't feel a blinding need to fill up the silence.

The silence was companionable. Maybe that was the sex. Whatever—it wasn't awkward for her any more.

'Airport?' Kent asked a moment later. 'Or night in a swanky hotel and airport in the morning?'

Sadie felt her heart rate pick up a little. One last night with Kent. She wasn't foolish enough to believe this was the start of something. As addictive as Kent could be, he had issues to get sorted. So did she. She needed to sort out what she wanted to do with her life and she didn't need the distraction of him.

She didn't want to trade one addiction for another.

'What, no spiders? No scorpions?'

Kent grinned. 'How will we manage?'

'Lead the way.'

Half an hour later they were opening the door to the executive suite at the Esplanade Central. Sadie brushed past Kent and threw herself on the cloudlike, king-sized bed, flapping about as if she were making a snow angel on the stark white bedding.

'Ah-h-h, bliss,' she murmured.

Kent looked at Sadie all stretched out and shook his head. 'Not yet.'

Sadie sucked in a breath at the undiluted lust she saw in the copper flecks of his eyes. She lifted her foot and placed it on his thigh. 'I need a shower first. I smell like Twisties.'

Kent's pulse tripped at getting Sadie wet all over. 'Good idea.' He pulled his T-shirt over his head. 'Get naked,' he said.

Sadie laughed even as the sight of his chest did funny things inside hers. 'I just need to put my laptop on charge,' she said.

He unzipped his jeans. 'Hurry.'

Sadie watched him as he headed to the shower until he disappeared from sight. Maybe getting on a plane tomorrow was going to be a little harder than she thought.

She vaulted off the bed at the unsettling thought. She grabbed her laptop out of her bag and set it up on the desk in the room, plugging it into the nearby power point. She opened the lid and pulled up the document from earlier. She took her memory stick out of the pouch in the laptop bag and was about to insert it when Kent called, 'Sadie Bliss, get your delectable butt in here now or I'm coming to get you.'

Sadie turned around to find a naked Kent standing in the doorway to the bathroom. She hadn't seen him naked and vertical and he really was a sight to behold. Even his deformed ankle didn't detract from his overwhelming masculinity. Her belly flopped and her heart did a painful squeeze.

She dropped the memory stick on the table and swallowed against her suddenly parched throat.

'Well, when you put it like that,' she said, mission forgotten as she kicked out of her shoes and lifted her T-shirt off as she walked towards him.

Kent grinned as he took three paces into the running shower, feeling the warmth hit the back of his neck, watching as Sadie entered the bathroom in just a tiny scrap of red and black fabric at the apex of her thighs, a foil packet between her teeth. His semi-arousal turned to full blown as she looked him straight in the eyes whilst she stripped the scrap away.

And when she stepped into the shower cubicle and sank straight to her knees he knew Sadie Bliss was going to be very hard to forget.

CHAPTER TEN

KENT was still grinning as he left Sadie washing her hair in the shower fifteen minutes later. This really wasn't how he thought this assignment was going to turn out.

He'd been prepared to tolerate it.

Tolerate her.

To have just pushed her against the shower tiles and had his way with her was not what he'd envisioned after their first not-so-promising shower incident in Cunnamulla.

Well, not seriously anyway.

His stomach growled and he remembered why he'd been kicked out of the shower. He picked up the room service menu off the bedside table and headed for the phone to order. He sat at the desk and dialed, shifting the open laptop to make room for the menu. Sadie's discarded memory stick sat next to it and he picked it up as he said, 'Hello,' into the receiver.

He had a brief conversation as he flicked through the menu ordering wildly inappropriate things that would probably give Tabitha apoplexy when the bill came in.

Champagne. Strawberries. Oysters. Cheese platter.

The fancy chocolate pudding with a warm gooey centre. He had definite plans for that.

His gaze fell on the laptop screen as he absently turned the memory stick over in his hands while the call taker repeated his order. The header *Kent Nelson, Mere Mortal* caught his eye and his grin faded.

He read the two paragraphs on the screen, then dropped the stick as he scrolled down further, replying automatically to the woman on the other end of the phone and hanging up, not hearing or caring if the order was correct.

He read it all—all two thousand words—his heart beating faster, anger simmering with every one. Everything he'd said, everything that had happened between them, was there. And more. Her observations. Her opinions.

Her pop psychology.

Stuff that he hadn't even begun to grapple with. Had shied from even thinking too hard about.

By the time he got to the end—*Kent Nelson is an enigma but no man is an island*—he was so mad he wanted to break things.

Sadie came out of the shower wrapped in a fluffy gown, towelling her hair. 'Did you order something?' she asked his back. 'I'm starving.'

Kent stood and turned to face her. 'You're writing a story about me?' he demanded.

Sadie frowned at the steel in his voice and the return of the hard lines of his face. She hadn't seen them for a couple of days now and had forgotten how austere they could be. 'No.'

He stepped aside and pointed to the laptop screen. 'I think you are.'

Sadie gasped as she realised what she'd done. She shook her head as she walked towards him. 'It's not what it looks like.'

Kent slashed his hand through the air, pulling her up short. 'I told you my story *was not* for sale. This stuff is private.'

Sadie struggled to understand how the day had gone

to hell so quickly. One moment they were in the shower and she was thinking she could get used to all that single-minded intensity of his, particularly when he was buried deep inside her, and the next he was looking at her with ice in his eyes.

Back to square one.

Sadie dropped the towel, her hair hanging in damp strips around her shoulders. 'I'm not doing a story on you. I'm just...journalling.'

'It sure as hell reads like a story,' he snapped. 'Did Tabitha put you up to this?' he demanded. 'She's been trying to get me to do an exclusive for months.'

Sadie took another step towards him but halted as he held out his hand. 'Tabitha has nothing to do with this. It's just me putting my thoughts and feelings down. I have absolutely no intention of doing anything with it. You can delete it right now if you want.'

Kent turned, leant over the keyboard and hit Control A. The article highlighted before his eyes and he hit the delete button.

He only wished it felt as satisfying as it looked.

Sadie watched her work disappear in dismay. Those words might have come easily but no writer liked to lose work. Sure, she could write them again, but they'd never be as perfect as they had been.

She propped her hands on her hips. 'Happy now?'

'Do you have a backup?' he asked.

Sadie nodded. 'On the memory stick.'

Kent picked up the stick. He gave her a wide berth as he rounded her and headed for the bathroom. Once inside he avoided looking at the shower cubicle as the memories of their soapy encounter returned. He strode to the toilet, opened the lid, tossed the stick in and flushed it.

'It's okay,' Sadie said derisively when he stormed out a

moment later, his limp more obvious than it had been in days. 'There wasn't anything important on there.'

Kent ignored her as he hefted his bag onto the bed and pulled out some clothes. Her apparent lack of concern over the loss of the article hadn't mollified him.

Had she been interviewing him all along? Was that what all the incessant questions had been about? Had she been taking notes the entire five days? Did she think that she could bat those incredible lashes at him and he wouldn't mean what he'd said yesterday—*God, was it only yesterday?*—that it was no one's damn business?

He'd thought she'd been joking about her interviewing him. Obviously not.

Sadie watched as he dressed quickly in jeans and a T-shirt, the flash of a naked back and buttocks when he dropped the towel having a funny effect on her pulse despite their current state of animosity. 'I'm not doing a story on you, Kent.'

Kent sat on the bed and stuffed his feet into his shoes. Whether she was or wasn't just wasn't the point any more. This debacle was a salient reminder of why he'd kept himself to himself.

He'd let Sadie Bliss and her treacherous curves get way too close. Her conjectures in the article had been searing and insightful and even now he shied from them.

He didn't want or need her inside his head. What the hell did someone in their mid-twenties know about stuff like this?

He'd come out here to get his photographic mojo back. Not to lose his head over a woman and certainly not to get it head shrunk by one either.

There were things he had to come to terms with, he knew that. But he was doing that to his own timetable.

She was wrong—this man was an island.

The uninhabitable kind.

He stood and looked at her. 'This was a mistake.'

Sadie blinked. 'What was? This hotel room? Sex in the shower? Sex on the roof of your car? Our night under the stars? Making me believe that I shouldn't be ashamed of my body? Talking about the accident? Or just the whole damn trip?'

Kent nodded, his jaw locked. 'All of it.' He should never have taken the assignment in the first place. He should have kept her at a distance.

His blunt admission rocked her back on her heels; she was surprised by how much it hurt. Okay, he was pissed at her. She got it. But did he really regret everything that had happened? Apart from this sticky end, which she would no doubt analyse ad nauseam in the coming months, she didn't have a one. Kent had helped her think differently about herself—about her body and her art.

And for that she would be for ever grateful.

'For the last time, I was not writing a story about you.'

Kent folded his arms across his chest. Okay, he believed her. But he doubted she was being honest with herself over her true reasons and that was cause for concern.

'Well, who were you writing it for?' he asked. 'Because if it was just for you then I think you may be a little…fixated on me.'

The last thing he needed was Sadie Bliss making his life difficult after they parted ways with some obsessive girly crush.

The last thing he needed was Sadie Bliss full stop.

'We had great sex, Sadie. But don't delude yourself—there can be nothing else.'

Sadie was speechless for a moment at the sheer ego on the man. She wished she could tell him it wasn't that good, but unfortunately she couldn't.

She could however assure him he wasn't the only man in the world. A girl had her pride.

'I hate to be the one to break this to you but I'm pretty sure you do not own the only penis-of-amazing-powers in the world and I'm *damn* sure I can get on with my life without pining for it.'

Although she'd probably think about it a little more than was healthy.

'Besides which,' she added, 'if you think all we had was sex, then maybe you're a little deluded. You shared stuff with me I'm betting you've never told anyone else. I can get sex and, thanks to you, I'll be sure to hold my future partners to a higher standard, but where are you going to find someone you can talk to, Kent? Because you *really* need to talk to someone.'

Kent glared at her, his face stony. He did not want to get into a conversation about his state of mind. That was especially none of her business. 'This is *not* about me, Sadie.'

'So you're just going to have nightmares for the rest of your life?' she demanded. 'You're going to hear poor Dwayne Johnson calling for his mother every time you shut your eyes?'

'I'll deal with my stuff,' he snapped. 'I just want to make sure you aren't spinning castles in the air because of our physical…intimacy.'

Sadie snorted. Kent had opened up so much from the guy he'd been at the beginning of the trip, but right now he'd taken a huge slide backwards. He couldn't even recognise they'd been more than just physically intimate. That there'd been emotional intimacy as well.

And he was running for the hills.

'Why on earth would I want to be involved with a man who is so guarded, so…' she floundered around looking for the most apt description that didn't involve mentioning how far up his backside his head was jammed '...deep in his man cave, I feel like I need a miner's lamp and pick whenever I talk to him? Relationships shouldn't be that hard, Kent.'

He nodded, his lips terse. *His work here was done.*

'Good,' he said, brushing past her and heading for the door. 'At least we agree on something.'

He was desperate to put as much distance as possible between him and her damn robe belt that was loosening and flashing glimpses of her cleavage. It made him want to throw her on the bed, which was not conducive to walking away.

To ending it.

Whatever *it* was.

Sadie turned and watched him limp away. 'Where are you going?' she asked.

He opened the door. 'Out.'

And then there was just Sadie left looking at a closing door, her heart beating wildly. She sank onto the end of the bed, her brain trying to catch up. Twenty minutes ago she'd had a screaming orgasm in the shower. Now Kent was gone and there was a heavy feeling in her chest and a growing urge to cry.

She stood. She would not cry. She'd cried over her father and cried over Leo.

She would not cry over a man she'd known for five days.

She walked on shaky legs to the telephone, ignoring the open laptop taunting her.

If only she'd shut the lid!

Maybe instead of scaring him off she and Kent would be talking right now about seeing each other some more. Because she hadn't been ready to say goodbye just yet and she was pretty damn sure, after that shower, he wasn't either.

She dialled the airport and changed her flight.

Six months later...

'C'mon.' Leila banged on the bathroom door. 'It's opening night and the gallery will be crowded.'

Sadie looked at herself one last time in the mirror. Why she was fussing she didn't know. He never went to gallery events, he'd told her that.

In fact she wouldn't normally be going either. Now she was a full-time student again she couldn't afford the big ticket price—she'd even had to take on a flatmate, Leila, to make the rent. But when two tickets had mysteriously turned up and Leila, a photography major, had spied them, Sadie hadn't had the heart to deny her.

And, truth be told, she was curious.

Sadie had already seen some of it, of course. The dozen photographs printed with her Leonard Pinto feature had been magnificent. But this exhibition, *Centre Attraction*, was the complete outback series and, being Kent's first exhibition of new work, had garnered a true buzz in the art scene.

It had been billed as *the* show to see.

'How do I look?' she asked Leila as she opened the door, her fingers absently stroking down the front of her retro fire-engine red dress. It dipped at the cleavage, nipped at the waist, clung to the hips and flared around the calves in an elegant fishtail.

'Woohoo, baby,' Leila crowed. 'I'd do you.'

Sadie laughed, the stress bunching her neck muscles instantly easing. Leila was out and proud and very much in a couple but her flattery was just what Sadie needed tonight. 'All right,' she said. 'Let's *do* this thing.'

Kent almost choked on his beer when he spotted Sadie sashay into the gallery. He hadn't been sure she'd come even with the tickets he'd sent her. And he certainly hadn't expected her to make such an entrance. The eyes of every straight man with a pulse tracked her path from the door to the bar area.

She'd come a long way since awful power suits and baggy T-shirts.

The gallery was crowded and he was stuck in a corner with some of Tabitha's cronies, but he watched her as she did the rounds of the displays. She chatted to the woman she'd arrived with and seemed to make polite conversation with other patrons who were admiring the exhibits as well.

None of them shone as she did.

Watching her felt like coming out of a fog and he realised he'd missed her even more than he'd thought. He'd wanted to see her, to show her his work that she'd been so much a part of. Particularly the centrepiece. He was proud of it and wanted her to be proud of it too.

But he hadn't expected everything to finally make sense by just looking at her.

Yes, he'd thought about her every day. Missed her every day. But this was more. So much more.

She was two exhibits away when he politely excused himself from the group of people he'd been barely paying attention to anyway.

Sadie stood in front of a photo of emus mid-dash across a western sky. The bounce of their soft feathers and the dust kicking up around their powerful legs gave the photograph a sense of motion and urgency. She remembered him taking the pictures. Telling her about his grandfather.

She studied it for a while as she waited for the crowd to clear from around the next piece. She'd been surreptitiously looking for him but he'd obviously been true to his word.

'Oh, my God.'

Sadie turned at the urgent tug on her arm administered by Leila. She wasn't too concerned though—Leila had been goggle-eyed all night, each photograph seemingly more fantastical through her rose-coloured glasses than the last.

'Sadie, is that you?'

Sadie frowned at her friend's face, then looked up at the photograph that had everyone's interest. It took a few seconds to compute what she was looking at and then everything inside her seemed to crash to a halt.

Her brain synapses. Her cellular metabolism.

The beat of her heart, the breath in her lungs.

It was the one he'd taken of her the night of the campfire. Where she'd stood and he'd called her name and she had looked back over her shoulder at him. It was a stunningly visual shot. Her face in shadow, her semi-naked body silhouetted in soft yellow light against a starry sky.

The caption read—*Sadie In The Sky With Diamonds*.

Beside it, enlarged and framed, was her sketch. The byline proclaiming her as the artist.

When she'd got home from Darwin she'd realised she'd left her sketch book in his car but hadn't bothered to contact him about it. A part of her had wanted him to have it, to have a tangible reminder of what they'd shared—*emotionally,* not physically.

Sadie could feel heat rising in her cheeks as she looked at it now. How could he share something so personal? How could he?

She'd believed him when he'd told her how very much he hadn't wanted *Mortality* to be shared. Had he not thought she'd feel the same way about this?

'You like?'

Sadie started at the oh-so-familiar tone. She turned to find him standing behind her, his mouth, beautiful as ever, so very, very close.

Her heart started again at the sight of him. It had been *so* long and he looked *so* good. Just as she remembered from the last long six months of thinking about him. Of sketching him.

Only better.

The dark suit blunted his *he-man* edge to a different kind of sexy and her belly clenched.

But it didn't change what he'd done or the sudden block of emotion welling in her chest. Her heart pounded in her ears as she shook her head. 'How could you?' she whispered, then pushed past him.

Away, she had to get away.

It was much harder for Kent to make his escape from the gallery than it had been for Sadie. He'd just caught a glimpse of her climbing into a taxi before someone blocked his view and it had been another twenty minutes before he'd managed to get away.

He guessed running out on your own exhibition was pretty poor form, but he'd only been there tonight hoping she'd show up.

And now she was gone, he didn't want to be there either.

He just wanted to be with her.

Luckily he knew the way to her flat and by the time he'd parked an hour had elapsed since she'd run from him.

'Sadie,' he called, knocking on her door. 'I know you're in there. Open up!'

Sadie, sitting in her daggy track pants and shirt, jumped at the harsh command. Her hand shook as she raised the glass of red wine to her lips.

Kent belted louder this time. 'I'm going to knock all night if I have to, Sadie!'

Sadie glared at the door. It was tempting to let him go

for it. Mrs Arbuthnot from next door called the police if a
cat meowed too loudly outside her door at night.

But she *was* pretty mad at him. And she did need to talk
to him about pulling the photo from the exhibition. She
stormed over to the door and pulled it open. 'You've got
a bloody nerve,' she said, turning on her heel and stomp-
ing back into the lounge room, leaving him standing on
the doorstep.

Kent shut the door after him and followed her at a more
sedate pace, finding her waiting for him, arms crossed,
grey eyes stormy, spoiling for a fight.

'I want it pulled,' she said straight up.

'Sadie—'

'No. You were supposed to delete those pictures. I did
not give you my permission to use a *half-naked* picture
of me in an exhibition that thousands of people will see.'

Kent undid his jacket buttons and thrust his hands on
his hips. 'But a fully naked portrait is perfectly fine?'

'What other ones have you used?' she demanded, ignoring his jibe. The portraits were consensual and he knew
it. 'Have you uploaded them somewhere? Damn it, Kent,
they're private and I want them back.' The words were familiar and a thought suddenly hit her. 'Oh, my God, that's
what this is about, isn't it? This is payback for that stuff I
wrote. For the last time, Kent, it *was not* a story!'

'Sadie,' Kent said, holding up a placating hand, trying not to be turned on by how gorgeous she was all het
up, her hair flying around her head, her eyes burning, her
chest rising and falling in an agitated rhythm.

'They're burned to a disc. I kept meaning to send them
to you but I couldn't bring myself to part with them. I
wouldn't share them with anyone.'

Sadie snorted. 'Just half of Sydney!'

'It's one photo, Sadie. No one knows it's you.'

'*I* know it's me!' she snapped. 'And let's not even mention the fact that you reproduced and displayed *my* artwork, without *my* permission!'

'The two pieces belong together.'

Sadie gaped. He didn't even look a little contrite, standing in her lounge room oozing sex and confidence in his important artist suit. She hadn't really expected to see him tonight and she resented how damn good he looked.

And how her traitorous body didn't seem to care that he'd just exposed something between them that had been intimate and private. He might as well have stripped her naked in front of everyone at the gallery.

'Why?' she demanded.

'Because it's a stunning image. The pick of all the photos I took on our road trip. Maybe one of the best of my career. And to apologise.'

Sadie blinked. 'Apologise?'

'For being such a prat in Darwin.'

'By being an even bigger prat now?' She gaped.

Kent saw the two spots of colour up high on her cheekbones and wanted to drag her into his arms so badly he had to grind his feet into the floor to stop himself from following through.

Sadie didn't look as if she was quite there yet.

He took a steadying breath. 'If you don't like it I'll have it withdrawn.'

Sadie sat down and took a gulp of her wine. She needed fortification. 'It's got nothing to do with not liking it,' she said slowly through clenched teeth.

'Okay,' he said, hands still on his hips as he looked down at her. 'Explain it to me. It's not like you haven't posed nude before, Sadie.'

'It's got nothing to do with that.' She glared up at him. 'That picture represents a very personal moment you and

I shared. And I know you're Mr I-don't-need-anybody and no doubt *he-men* pander to women with poor self-image every day, but it means something to me. I feel about it the way you feel about *Mortality*. That photo is an intensely private moment. Not for public viewing. It's not my body I want to protect. It's the moment.'

Kent sat down on the coffee table behind him, his legs stretching out, almost touching hers. He was encouraged when she didn't attempt to move away. 'I'll have it withdrawn first thing tomorrow,' he murmured.

Sadie looked into the multi-hues of brown that made up his eyes. 'Thank you.'

Kent nodded, his heart thudding as her gaze locked with his. 'It's good to see you, Sadie Bliss.'

She shook her head. 'Don't.'

He half smiled. 'Don't what?'

'I'm not going to fall into bed with you because you turn up on my doorstep all sexy and apologetic. I'm still mad.'

He chuckled then. 'I missed you.'

Sadie sipped at her wine, determined not to give him an inch. 'Yeh, well, I haven't missed you,' she lied.

'I've thought about you every day, Sadie. And I've pretended that's a lot of things—fond memories, lust, friendship—but I saw you tonight and I knew it was more than that.' He dropped his gaze to her full mouth that had parted as she listened. He wanted to kiss her so badly he could almost taste her. 'You're under my skin, Sadie Bliss.'

Sadie's internal muscles undulated deep down inside her at his words and his sudden intense look. It would be so easy to just throw caution to the wind and hurl herself at him, but after six months apart she knew two things.

She was head first in love with him. And the Kent she knew couldn't handle that.

'I'm back at art school,' she said as his gaze returned

to her face. 'I'm loving it. For the first time in my life I really know what I want to do. I'm actually my own person. I love you, Kent. I think I have from the moment you let me drive the Land Rover.'

She paused. Her pulse was beating triple time but the admission had been surprisingly easy to make.

'But I can't take on your stuff. I need to be in a relationship where I can talk with the other person, where no subject is off limits, no words are left unsaid. Where I can talk whenever I want to. I have a lot to say.' She smiled at her own joke. 'I'm prepared to do some hard yards but I need to know that you're going to meet me halfway.'

Kent knew what she was saying was true. 'How did you get to be so wise so young?' he asked.

Sadie smiled around her wine glass. 'Misspent youth.'

Kent placed his hands on his knees. 'I've been seeing a psychologist for the last four months. It's been…hard at times. But it's helped. I've started to write a memoir about the time I was embedded. I even went on a commercial flight just recently. The dream doesn't come so much any more.'

He paused. Smiled at her. 'Now all I usually dream about is you.' She smiled back at him and he felt encouraged. 'I can't promise I'm going to be happiness and light twenty-four seven but my life didn't make sense for a long time and then you came along and, briefly, it did. I don't know how our future is going to pan out, Sadie—I'm so happy that you're pursuing your art dream and at some stage I'm going to want to take another overseas assignment—but I know that whatever happens I want you in it. I love you, Sadie.'

Sadie considered him over the rim of the glass, her heart beating frantically at words that were like music to her ears. The man who had taught her to embrace who she was, to glory in it, was telling her he loved her.

'That's all I need,' she murmured.

Kent held her gaze. He wasn't sure what that meant. Or whose move it was.

Sadie sat forward, placing her wine glass on the table beside him. 'So,' she said, resting her bent elbow on her knee and propping her chin on her palm, 'these dreams? Do I have my clothes on?'

Okay, Sadie's move. He grinned. 'Not often.'

'Are they…graphic?'

Kent nodded. 'Usually.'

She reached for his tie and started to untie the knot. 'I think you're going to have to demonstrate,' she murmured.

Kent nuzzled her temple, her ear, her neck. 'I'm good at demonstrating.'

Sadie slid the tie out from the collar with a loud zip. She stood, his tie dangling from her finger. 'Well come on then, let's get started.'

She held out her hand and he took it.

* * * * *

LET'S TALK
Romance

For exclusive extracts, competitions
and special offers, find us online:

f facebook.com/millsandboon

◎ @millsandboonuk

🐦 @millsandboon

Or get in touch on 0844 844 1351*

For all the latest titles coming soon, visit
millsandboon.co.uk/nextmonth

Want even more
ROMANCE?

Join our bookclub today!

'Mills & Boon books, the perfect way to escape for an hour or so.'

Miss W. Dyer

'Excellent service, promptly delivered and very good subscription choices.'

Miss A. Pearson

'You get fantastic special offers and the chance to get books before they hit the shops'

Mrs V. Hall

Visit millsandbook.co.uk/Bookclub and save on brand new books.

MILLS & BOON